BIDDING FOR THE BACHELOR

FONG BROTHERS, BOOK 2

JACKIE LAU

First edition: August 2021
ISBN: 978-1-989610-25-1

Editor: Latoya C. Smith, LCS Literary Services

Cover Design: Flirtation Designs

Cover photograph: Adobe Stock

[1]

CEDRIC

"A BACHELOR AUCTION?" I say.

"Haven't you heard of these before?" Po Po asks. "I read about one in a book and suggested it to your father. He said it was a good idea." She smiles proudly as she helps herself to the fried rice.

My grandmother might be excited about this, but I have a sinking feeling.

My family runs the Toronto Chinese Canadian Center, and every February, there's a gala to raise money for it. And apparently this year, the gala will include a bachelor auction.

I can see exactly where this is going.

Both my brothers, Julian and Vince, are married, and as the last single Fong, I will be expected to take part in it.

We're at my parents' house for dinner tonight. Everyone is here: my parents, my grandma, Julian, Vince, their wives, and their kids.

"We thought you could be in the auction," Mom says to me.

And there it is.

"It'll be fun!" Vince, asshole that he is, can't help smirking. "Think of all the money you'll make for charity. You've seen

Groundhog Day? One of the winning bids was a whole twenty-five cents. I'm sure you'll make at least five dollars."

"The gala is on February 13 this year," Dad says. "The next day is Valentine's Day, so the idea is that you spend Valentine's Day with the person who bids for you."

"Or their children," Vince chimes in. "I'm sure many people will be bidding for their adult children and grandchildren."

"Who knows?" says Courtney, Julian's wife. "You might even find true love."

I'm not against love, but in this situation, it seems highly unlikely. Plus, even though I could see myself getting married one day, it's far from my priority right now.

My first priority is finding a new apartment. I currently live in a small one-bedroom in a condo building downtown, not far from the college where I teach. However, my landlord sold my unit, and the new owner isn't renting the place but living there himself. I need to be out by the beginning of March.

Fun times.

Not.

Rent is expensive in Toronto, and I haven't been able to find anything as good.

If I can't get a new apartment, I can move back in with my parents temporarily, but I would prefer not to do that. I'm used to having my freedom, and I don't think it would be good for my writing.

I haven't written a great deal in years, but that's my other priority. Finally writing another novel.

Dating and bachelor auctions? Not so much.

Last year, I put some effort into dating, then got discouraged and deleted all the apps off my phone. I'll try again one day, but not yet.

I look at my brothers. I could ask someone in my family for financial help—I wouldn't need a ton—but, no. I have my pride.

"So, will you do it?" Mom asks. "We've already got seven guys lined up, and we also asked Sam Leung, though I doubt he'll agree. But you'd be a big draw."

She says this not because she's my mother and she's biased, but because my family is well-known in the Chinese community here.

Or maybe for both reasons.

I shake my head. "Sorry, I think I'll pass."

"Cedric!" Po Po's lower lip trembles. "You are thirty-six. Getting old. I want you to settle down with a nice woman—or other person—before I drop dead."

I smile at her. When I came out to my family last year, she was initially rather quiet, which is unusual for my grandma. But two days later, she insisted on setting me up with her friend's grandson. I didn't need the unsolicited matchmaking, but still. I felt lucky.

"I'll find someone eventually," I say.

"Don't wait too long! I am ninety-two. You think I will live another ten years?"

"Actually, I do, Ma," my mother says.

Po Po sniffs. "Cedric, if you do not participate in this bachelor auction, I will come to your apartment and blast Chinese opera music until it hurts your ears."

I sip my tea. "How lovely."

She leans toward my little niece. "Don't you think Uncle Cedric should be in the bachelor auction?"

Evie giggles from her high chair and holds up her spoon. "All done!"

"That means yes."

"Yes!" Evie says gleefully.

"You see?"

"Stop putting my daughter in the middle of your arguments," Julian says.

"It is not an argument," Po Po protests. "We are just having a polite discussion, yes?"

Mom puts down her chopsticks. "In the auction booklet—"

"Booklet?" I choke.

"Well, it's not really a booklet, but a sheet of paper about your age and profession and such. Anyway, it mentions who is allowed to bid for you. We'll say anyone is allowed to bid for you, not just women? Your choice. We do have a gay man…"

"Is this Alvin?" Alvin is Po Po's friend's grandson.

"Yes!" Po Po says. "You should be a good grandson like him. What else will you do on Valentine's Day? Might as well spend it meeting someone new."

I turn to my brothers. "Valentine's Day. Anyone need babysitting? I'm free."

"Nah." Vince folds his arms over his chest. "I'd rather see you go on a date."

"Courtney's mother is taking care of Evie for the weekend," Julian says, "so we can go to the gala and have a Valentine's lunch together."

"If you don't want to do this, Cedric," Dad says, "it's fine. I won't force you."

"But I will bribe you!" Po Po holds up her hand. "If you do the auction, I will give you two hundred dumplings."

"Are you buying these dumplings from the store?" I ask. "Or making them yourself?"

"Homemade."

The table falls silent.

Because my grandmother's dumplings are, well, *everything*.

She used to make them regularly, but she hasn't made them in years. When she reached ninety, she decided it was time to stop spending so much time in the kitchen.

And two hundred of them…

"Can I participate in this auction?" Vince asks.

Marissa, his wife, shoots him a glare. "You're married."

"I'd do it just for the dumplings. Don't worry, nothing would happen. Or you could bid on me."

"This offer is for Cedric only," Po Po says.

"Not fair," Vince mutters.

"How about me?" Dad asks. "Can I do it?"

Evie, not wanting to be left out, shouts, "Me!"

"So, what do you think?" Po Po looks at me. "Either I play high-volume Chinese opera music, or I give you two hundred dumplings. Easy choice, yes?"

I nod. It *is* an easy choice.

I'm a sucker for dumplings.

In fact, this now sounds like a great deal, one I'm eager to take. The idea of being the center of attention at the gala is a bit awkward, but it's worth it for the dumplings.

"I'll do it."

As I say the words, a thrill of excitement spreads through me. Who might bid on a date with me? Maybe it'll turn out well.

Why am I suddenly hopeful?

I need to focus on my apartment and writing a novel, but apparently my inner romantic has made a surprise appearance.

Po Po beams at me. "You are the best grandson."

"Excuse me?" Vince says.

"And you are all so easily manipulated with food."

"You're one to talk," Mom says. "I only got you to the optometrist because I bribed you with chestnut cake."

"Chestnut cake?" Marissa perks up. "Where?"

"Not my fault it's so tasty!" Po Po says. "But I'm still mad you ate a slice."

"You wanted the whole cake to yourself?" Mom asks. "You ate at least half of it. That wasn't enough?"

Evie bangs her spoon on the tray of the high chair. "Cake!"

"Yes, love," Courtney says. "You're a little cake monster, aren't you?"

Yeah, yeah, cake is delicious, but have you tried my grandmother's dumplings?

I can't wait.

[2]

BRIAN

THIS IS A MESS, and I love it.

I don't know what the Fongs were thinking. A charity bachelor auction? We're only on the second bachelor, and already two fistfights have nearly broken out.

It doesn't help that this man, Kelvin Kwong, truly has it all.

First of all, he's a doctor, because of course he is, plus he's tall and handsome. Not to my taste, but I know a lot of people would find him attractive.

And, oh yeah, he's an astronaut.

A fucking doctor *and* an astronaut?

His parents are probably insufferable with all the bragging they do. I bet his parents' friends say to their underachieving kids, *Why can't you be more like Kelvin? He's an astronaut now, did you hear?*

Because let me tell you, that's what my parents would do.

I tense at the thought of my parents. We're no longer on speaking terms.

But then Carrie Lo laughs and whispers, "Look at the table beside us."

A middle-aged man is trying to stop a woman—presumably

his wife—from putting up her bidding paddle, while a younger woman is shaking her head. Their daughter, I'm guessing.

"Fourteen thousand?" Vince Fong says. "Do I hear fourteen thousand?"

Someone holds up their paddle.

I once considered Vince my closest friend, but I haven't seen him in months. He's busy with his wife and a baby now, but that's not the main reason we haven't met up.

Seeing him on stage, wearing a tux and acting as the auctioneer for the evening… Well, it does cause a slight twinge, but not as much as I expected.

Perhaps because I'm too amused by the shitshow taking place.

I've attended this gala every year since I met Vince. This year, I figured I'd still go to show my support for his family's charity, and I got my friend Carrie to come with me. We've been having a good time, drinking a decent amount of wine. We don't know anyone else at our table, but that's okay.

"Fifteen thousand," Vince says. "Do I hear fifteen thousand?"

A woman starts to hold up her paddle, but she's tackled by an elderly lady. There's a bunch of shouting. Security intervenes.

It's almost midnight and many people are tipsy. Perhaps they should have held the bachelor auction at the beginning of the evening.

But this is great entertainment. Better than the singer who performed earlier.

I never used to lack for entertainment in my life. I was always traveling and having parties at my ginormous house.

And then my dad cut me off.

I sold the mansion, bought a condo in Yorkville, and am living off the rest of the proceeds from the sale. Which is quite a bit—I'm lucky—but nothing like what I'm used to.

With everything that happened, I'm not in the mood for as much partying anyway, but don't get me wrong. I still have fun. I still have sex—this afternoon, for example, I met up with

Gabriella. But some of my friends, who were really only around because of my over-the-top, expensive lifestyle, have lost interest. I suppose they weren't really friends.

Fortunately, I do have people who give a shit or two about me. Like Carrie. Her attention is diverted from the auction as Marissa approaches our table.

"It's so good to see you!" Carrie exclaims as they hug. "How are you? How's Lucas?"

"This is the longest I've been away from him," Marissa says. "It's so strange. I have to stop myself from texting my mom every half hour."

"I'm sure he's fine with her. Tell him that Auntie Carrie will visit next weekend! The video you sent me yesterday was *so* adorable."

Marissa turns and acknowledges me. "Hey, Brian."

She and I haven't gotten the opportunity to know each other well. I mean, it's kind of awkward—she has what I want.

I'm not talking about the baby.

That's the main reason I don't hang out with Vince anymore: I confessed my feelings for him, and he shot me down. Unsurprising, since he'd just shown me the ring he'd bought for Marissa. Plus, he only likes women.

It's rather uncomfortable to see him after that confession, and I figure keeping my distance will help me get over him. Besides, our lives are a lot different than they were when we hung out all the time.

"Sixteen thousand it is," Vince says up on stage. "Congrats, you've won a date with Kelvin Kwong!"

The woman in question looks particularly pleased.

"And now for our next bachelor. At the age of twenty-four, he founded…"

Turns out this bachelor is some kind of self-made tech guy.

"What do you think?" Carrie whispers to me. Marissa has returned to her table.

"Meh," I say.

The other people at our table, however, are furiously whispering. I can't make out everything because they're speaking in Mandarin and my Mandarin isn't as good as it should be. A young woman, her mom, and her grandma, from the looks of it. It seems like Mom wants to bid and Daughter is resistant to the idea.

"For eight thousand dollars, I'd rather go to Paris!" she suddenly bursts out.

While they're arguing, the bidding continues, and an elderly woman wins. A date for her granddaughter, or for herself?

The next poor bachelor—how did these guys get roped into this?—is another doctor, and he looks quite spiffy in his suit and seems to enjoy being the center of attention. He spins around and dances to the music that begins playing, then strikes a pose at the end.

His name is Alvin, and only men are allowed to bid on him.

When this is announced, a middle-aged woman makes a disapproving sound, and I glare at the back of her head.

"He's pretty cute, no?" Carrie says to me.

"Yeah, he's kinda cute." Not that I have any intention of bidding on anyone tonight. A date for Valentine's is not what I need.

A bidding war escalates between two young men. One is sitting in the front by himself; the other is at a table near us, being egged on by his parents.

The first man finally wins, and we move on to the next bachelor, who is a professor of economics, interested in women.

I flip through the booklet to see how many bachelors there are and who's up next. When I get to the last page, I feel a strange jolt.

Cedric Fong. Globe and Mail bestselling author...

Vince's brother is in the bachelor auction.

I shouldn't be surprised. Of course the Fongs would want him to participate.

At the bottom of the page, it says that anyone is allowed to bid on a date with Cedric. Interesting. I hadn't realized Cedric wasn't straight. Though I'd briefly wondered, when I saw him at a café last year…

The next bachelor makes a grand entrance, twirling his suit jacket over his head, followed by sexily removing his tie.

I perk up. How far will he go?

I'm impressed when he starts unbuttoning his shirt as he swings his hips back and forth, He drops the shirt to the floor and stands there in a white tank top and dress pants.

"This is inappropriate," mutters one of the elderly women at the table next to me, but the woman beside her is staring raptly at what's unfolding on stage.

The man is getting lots of cheers. Many people seem to be into this, and I don't blame them. He's kinda hot. He gestures for people to give him more applause, and they do, me included.

And then the stripping bachelor puts his hands on the hem of his tank top.

Vince cuts him off. "Alright, Pythagoras. This is a family event."

Pythagoras?

That's his name?

Poor guy. At least my mom had the good sense to name me "Brian" in English. I once met a guy named "Harvard."

He ended up going to Yale.

Just kidding. He went to York University and almost flunked out because he was partying all the time. He went by "Harvey."

Pythagoras apparently goes by "Perry."

I don't blame him.

Having been told not to go any further, he flexes his bicep and kisses it, which is kind of a douche move, but whatever. He's got nice muscles. He can get away with shit like this.

I gulp my wine as I watch the show.

Yep, definitely more entertaining than last year's gala.

"Let's start the bidding at five hundred dollars," Vince says. "Do I hear five hundred?"

The bids quickly escalate.

"Look!" Carrie points to the far end of the room, where one woman is holding up her cane, and a young man is trying to stop her from smacking another woman.

Security rushes in.

Eventually, she's dragged out, and someone successfully wins a date with Perry.

The next bachelor is a doctor who isn't named after some ancient Greek dude.

The mom across from us is furiously whispering. "Very handsome! He will make nice babies. And unlike the last one, he is not a show-off!"

I give the daughter a look of sympathy.

They don't bid on a date with the doctor, but then it's Cedric's turn.

He comes out from behind the curtain and merely waves. No dancing for Cedric Fong. And no stripping, either.

Pity.

"Last but not least," Vince says, "my brother Cedric!" He walks across the stage and gives Cedric a hearty slap on the shoulder. "I'll give you a quick run-down of his accomplishments, but if you find me later, I'll tell you the good stuff. The embarrassing stories."

People laugh, and usually I'd be looking at Vince, but my eyes are drawn to Cedric. He looks the tiniest bit uncomfortable up there, but he's pretty cute.

I'd thought that before, and it's not due to his resemblance to Vince—because there's little resemblance. Cedric looks more like Julian, their older brother, and Julian isn't my type. Too serious and stuffy. Vince tried to bring Julian to one of my parties back in the day, and Julian totally lost his shit.

Strange that I keep looking at Cedric when Vince is right there, though.

"He's a Fong," the mom across from me hisses at her daughter. "We're bidding."

"No!"

"Wah, they are so rich and influential!"

"And he is sexy," the grandmother says. She switches to English for the last word.

The daughter covers her face with her hands.

I try not to laugh.

The bidding begins. There are several people interested, but once it hits ten thousand, there are only two groups of people bidding, one headed by the mother sitting across from me.

At the table next to us, a side bet is going on. Two elderly men are betting on who's going to win. I consider starting a similar bet with Carrie.

"Twelve thousand," Vince says. "Do I hear twelve thousand?"

But as time passes, the poor daughter at my table looks more and more uncomfortable, and I don't feel right about making any side bets. She's pleading with her mom to stop, but the mom isn't having any of it.

Carrie and I look at each other.

"The poor girl," Carrie murmurs.

"Thirteen thousand," Vince says. "Anyone for thirteen thousand?"

Before I know what I'm doing, I grab my bidding paddle. "Twenty thousand."

Everyone looks at me.

There are a few seconds of complete silence.

"Twenty-one thousand? Do I hear twenty-one thousand? Going once, going twice…"

Nobody speaks, although the mother and grandmother across the table are giving me dirty looks.

"I didn't see that coming," says one of the men making side bets. "Mind you, I didn't predict the strip show, either."

"Congratulations!" Vince says. "You just won a date with Cedric Fong."

The daughter looks at me and mouths, "Thank you."

[3]

CEDRIC

Brian Poon.

I have a Valentine's Day date with *Brian Poon*?

When I agreed to be in the bachelor auction, I certainly never expected my brother's ex-best friend to bid. It's not like Brian has any shortage of people interested in him. He goes out and has people in his bed all the time.

Unlike me.

I walk off the stage and sit down at my family's table. Dad takes the microphone, thanks everyone for coming, and announces there will be a bit of dancing to end the night.

I don't intend to participate, but then I see Brian walking over to our table.

Oh, shit, does he want to dance?

He pulls up an empty chair and sits backward on it, arms crossed over top. He manages to look suave while doing so.

"Tomorrow," he says. "You wanna start by grabbing dim sum?"

I'm not attracted to Brian because, well…that's just the way things are. The way I am. Yet I clearly remember the first time I saw him, when he was leaving Vince's old penthouse. There was something about him that intrigued me, I guess?

Which I don't get.

I've heard a bunch about Brian Poon over the years, and I feel like I have a pretty good understanding of who he is. He's all about going out, having a good time, and throwing his money around.

His actions tonight fit what I know of him.

Except…

"Why me?" I ask.

He gives a casual shrug. "The people across from me who were bidding… Well, the daughter looked very uncomfortable. Figured I'd put an end to her misery."

Though he speaks as though it's no big deal, he just spent twenty thousand dollars.

Twenty fucking thousand dollars!

Yes, my family is rich and my brothers have done well for themselves. But me? Not so much. One somewhat-successful novel does not a fortune make.

Brian's answer piques my curiosity, though. It sounds like he did this for someone he didn't know, and it's not what I would have expected of him.

"Anyway," he says. "I figure we'll eat some good food, hang out, grab a few drinks. That okay with you?"

It sounds like he doesn't really see this as a date.

I'm relieved. Because Brian is nothing like me. In many ways, he's the opposite, and I can't see us working out at all.

Plus, he's in love with my brother. Or, at least, he used to be. Vince revealed that to me recently.

"Yep," I say. "Sounds good."

After flashing me a smile, Brian walks to the back of the room with a swagger.

"Not sure I approve of this," Po Po says from beside me.

It's well after midnight. How on earth is she so perky? She's ninety-two! I'm fifty-six years younger than her, and I'm yawning.

"Brian Poon is bad news." She makes a face. "Do you want to turn into Vince?"

"What's so bad about turning into me?" Vince asks with faux innocence. "I'm awesome, and I have a wife and a baby—you like that, don't you?"

"Wah, you know what I mean. What you *used* to be like. Next thing you know, Cedric will be doing lines of cocaine off a woman's stomach!"

We stare at my grandma.

"Sorry," Po Po says. "It could be a man. Or—"

"Po Po," Vince says, "where did you get this idea?"

"Ah, I saw it in a movie recently. I'm old, what else do I have to do all day? Yesterday, I watched three movies."

An awful thought occurs to me.

"You don't approve of my Valentine's date," I say slowly. "Does this mean you won't make dumplings for me?"

"What are you talking about? I said I would make you one hundred dumplings if you participated in this auction. You participated, you get dumplings."

I can't believe what I'm hearing. "You promised me *two* hundred dumplings, and now you're saying only one hundred?"

Po Po frowns. "Is that what I said? No, I think you must be trying to trick your poor grandmother."

My mom approaches, shaking her head. "Your grandma is teasing you. She made the dumplings this week, all two hundred of them. I saw her. When I tried to help, she yelled at me."

"Because you have no skills. I am the one with the dumpling skills." Po Po turns back to me. "You will get them on Monday, don't worry. I won't give them to you before your date because I don't want Brian to steal them. I don't trust that man."

"You think he'd steal my dumplings?" I ask.

"Maybe that is the only reason he bid on a date with you!"

"He told me—"

"No," Vince said. "Brian wouldn't pay twenty thousand dollars for a chance to steal two hundred dumplings from Cedric. That's a hundred dollars a dumpling—"

"Are you saying my dumplings aren't worth it?" Po Po demands.

"—and I don't think he knows about the dumplings. And yes, your dumplings are very good, but not *that* good."

"What if I put marijuana in them? They would be like, how do you say, edibles?"

Vince turns to Mom. "What on earth is she watching?"

Po Po sniffs. "I bet Brian Poon knows about the dumplings. He has put a secret microphone in our house and can hear everything!"

"Was this in the movie with men snorting cocaine off women's stomachs?" Mom asks.

Vince doubles over in laughter. "Alright, everyone. As fun as this is, I need to get home with my wife." He nods in the direction of Marissa, who has fallen asleep on her chair. A fond smile graces his lips as he stands up.

Po Po drags her chair closer to me. "I have been thinking. You have not been writing much, yes? Maybe the problem is that you don't have enough good ideas. Now that I am done making dumplings, I have a new mission! I will come up with ideas for you."

"Thanks, but I'm really—"

"Don't you think marijuana dumplings are smart?" She's whispering now, as if afraid other people will overhear her brilliant suggestions. "Could be about badass grandma trying to pay off her grandson's med school debt."

"Um…" I don't know how to respond to this.

My gaze wanders across the room. I see Vince talking to Brian near the exit.

Vince gestures in my direction, and I can't help wondering what he's saying.

[4]

BRIAN

"Don't you dare screw around with my brother," Vince says.

It's rare to hear him angry like this.

I cross my arms over my chest and lean casually against the wall. "What do you think I'm going to do?"

"I don't know. Fuck him and break his heart?"

Once upon a time, I told Vince that I thought Cedric was rather cute, to get under his skin when I learned he was in love with Marissa.

I won't lie, at least not to myself. If I'd gotten the sense that Cedric was interested, I'd be quite happy to have Valentine's Day sex, but I didn't feel any chemistry between us, so instead, we'll hang out for the day.

To my surprise, I'm rather excited about it.

Vince's lack of trust rankles, but at the same time, it's sweet that he's protective. My own brother would never worry about my well-being.

I sigh. "I promise. Nothing will happen between me and Cedric."

Vince's face relaxes and he slaps my back.

It feels like old times…almost.

The following day, I drive to Cedric's apartment to pick him up.

"Where are you taking me?" he asks as we get on the Don Valley. He sounds the tiniest bit alarmed.

I shoot him a grin before returning my attention to the road.

"Dim sum," I say. "As promised."

Fifteen minutes later, he says, "Surely we don't have to go this far for good dim sum."

"It's not *good*. It's the best. The place where my mom and I always used to go in Richmond Hill."

"Is that where you grew up?" he asks.

"Yeah."

Perhaps I'm overselling it. It's quality food, yes, but the only reason it's the best for me is because of nostalgia, and I've been wanting to go here for a while.

But dim sum isn't the sort of thing I do alone, and although I have a nice group of friends, we mostly hang out at the bar. I last had dim sum with Carrie, but she'd never trek all the way out to Richmond Hill. She rarely goes more than a few blocks north of Bloor, let alone Steeles.

Since I paid twenty thousand dollars for the privilege of spending the day with Cedric, he's coming to Richmond Hill.

As we walk inside the large restaurant, it's like I've come home, yet at the same time, I feel a sadness that I've never felt here before.

Growing up, it was just my mother and me. Yes, I have a father and a brother and a sister, but my siblings are several years older. When they were younger, my whole family lived in Hong Kong, and then my siblings were shipped off to boarding school on the other side of the world. Ma and I moved to Canada when I was five, and I attended private school here, but once I was in university, she moved back to Hong Kong.

To be honest, I'm glad I didn't grow up around my father and brother. They're terrible people, and we never spoke all that much, so I don't miss them now.

My mother, however…

Luckily, once we start eating, it's hard to focus on anything but the food because it's just so delicious.

The fung jao here is the best in the whole world. And this isn't just childhood nostalgia talking. We have to get a second order, as Cedric and I demolish the first order of chicken feet in a matter of minutes.

Cedric pops a piece of cheong fun into his mouth, and my gaze, not for the first time, is drawn to his lips. I have all sorts of dirty thoughts about what I'd like to see him do with those lips, but I have every intention of keeping them to myself.

First of all, because I promised Vince.

And second of all, because Cedric has shown no such interest in me.

I notice he's finished his tea, so I pour us each some more before saying, "Did the bachelor auction go the way your family expected?"

"You mean, did we anticipate multiple fights, all instigated by old women? No."

I can't help laughing. "I hope you do this every year. It was excellent entertainment."

"We raised a lot of money. In part thanks to you."

I shrug. "How did your family manage to find an astronaut doctor?"

"Julian knows him," Cedric says. "Kelvin is probably used to having women thrown in his direction by Chinese mamas. A bachelor auction was just another day for him. Making the rest of us feel inferior."

At least Cedric wrrote a book and has a job.

Me, on the other hand?

My life has felt particularly pointless lately. Not that I wish I'd gone to med school, then applied to be an astronaut—I wouldn't have gotten in, anyway—but now I wish I'd done something more than just having fun.

My life has no purpose, other than pissing off my family.

"How'd they get you to participate in the auction?" I ask. "Did they threaten to share embarrassing childhood photos?"

"No, but my grandma is delivering two hundred homemade dumplings to me tomorrow."

"You sold yourself out for dumplings?"

He inclines his head with a little half-smile. "They're very good dumplings, and she rarely makes them."

I totally understand being motivated by dumplings. "Since I made the winning bid, do I get half these dumplings?"

"She was quite clear that you're not supposed to have any."

"She doesn't like me?"

"Well, she doesn't trust you."

I put a hand to my heart. "I'm offended."

Despite my sarcastic tone, something else must have shown on my face, because Cedric feels the need to reassure me.

"It's not like she knows you at all," he says.

"My reputation precedes me."

"She thinks you were a bad influence on Vince, but I'm sure he was a bad influence on himself."

"Cheers." I hold up my teacup.

Cedric laughs, and the way his eyes crinkle is very appealing.

Yeah, there are definitely worse ways to spend Valentine's.

[5]

CEDRIC

AT NINE O'CLOCK THAT NIGHT, Brian and I are sitting side by side at a small table in Lychee, a restaurant and lounge on Elizabeth Street.

It's obvious that nearly everyone around us is on a date. It's Valentine's Day after all, and there are lots of tables of two. Some people probably assume we're on a date, too, but thankfully, it hasn't felt at all like a date today, and spending time with Brian is surprisingly…normal.

I had a larger-than-life image of him in my head. Even when he told me last night that we'd just eat, drink, and hang out today, I didn't imagine it would be that simple. Not with him.

But it is.

We started with dim sum, and then he took me to a Hong Kong dessert place, where we both got mango pomelo sago. Afterward, he drove us back downtown and parked his car at a building in Yorkville—does he own a second place in Yorkville? I didn't ask. We had coffee, followed by lobster at a restaurant in Chinatown. He insisted on paying, and hey, if he wanted to treat me to lobster for dinner, that was fine with me.

And now we're having cocktails upstairs at Lychee. Given the name of this place, I decided to get one of two cocktails with lychee in them. This one also has gin, and some other things that I forget. Whatever it is, it's very good. Brian is having the same drink, and when he ordered, he requested a particular type of gin for both of us. Probably something expensive that's wasted on me, but I'm not complaining.

It's nice to have someone planning everything. That sort of thing takes a lot of mental energy for me, but Brian seems to have endless ideas, and he always asks me if everything is okay, and it always is.

Yeah, today is going better than expected.

"Hey, Brian," one of the waiters calls out as he walks by.

Brian lifts a hand in greeting.

"You come here often?" I ask.

"Fairly often," he says. "When I want to have a drink alone in the middle of the week."

I frown. "It's a long way from where you live, isn't it?"

"It's about a half-hour walk, which I don't mind."

"The place where you parked your car in Yorkville…is that where you live now? I figured it was just a place to crash when you were downtown for the night."

He laughs. "You thought I was still on the Bridle Path?"

Yeah. I'd heard stories about his gigantic house with fountains and even a tennis court and hedge maze.

"I moved to my condo six months ago," he says. "After my dad cut me off for being, you know." He gestures between us. This isn't a real *date*, but I know what he's getting at.

"Shit," I say. "I'm sorry."

"That I'm not quite as filthy rich as before? Yeah, having a three-bedroom condo in Yorkville is rough."

I give him a look.

He responds by having a long swallow of his drink. "You're probably surprised my dad didn't already know. I told my mom I was bi when I was seventeen, but she made me swear not to tell my dad, so I didn't. Took longer than expected for it to get back to him." Brian chuckles. "He likely heard rumors but brushed them off until he was shown photographic evidence."

Seventeen.

I definitely didn't know anything when I was seventeen.

I'm not sure what to say. I—

"The waiters here are hot, don't you think?" He knocks his shoulder against mine.

"Uh, yeah. They are." I've had practice at faking these conversations over the years, but for some reason, I don't sound convincing today.

"You don't think so?"

I haven't been out very long, and Brian likely assumes I'm uncomfortable talking about men in this way, even if I'm on a not-quite-date with another guy. But it's more complicated than that.

Fortunately, he moves the conversation forward, which he's good at doing.

"Any plans for tomorrow?" he asks.

"My family is bringing over my dumplings, and I'm checking out a few apartments. I need to be out of my current place by the end of the month."

"That sucks."

"It does." I pause. "I write better with peace and quiet and no distractions, and if I moved in with my parents and grandmother, they'd be endlessly interrupting. So that's not an option, if I can help it."

"What are you working on now?"

"Um."

"I read that second novels are always hard," he says.

"It wouldn't really be a second novel. I mean, I wrote three novels before the one I sold."

"So, you're working on your fifth novel now?"

"I've started seven in the past few years, but I can never get past chapter five."

At least I've managed to write some short stories in the last year, but anything more than four thousand words eludes me. I never used to be like this, and it's frustrating.

"Do you want to write more?" he asks. "If you don't, that's cool, you can find something else to do with your life."

"I want to—I've wanted to be a writer since I was a child—yet I never end up doing it."

"I get it. That applies to me and, well, lots of things."

In addition to being easier to hang out with than expected, I'm beginning to suspect there are hidden depths to Brian Poon.

At ten o'clock, the lights dim, and Brian sports a grin as one of the waiters comes around and hands out new menus. Just a single sheet of drinks.

"Their late-night menu," Brian says. "Though I object to the idea of ten o'clock being late. But this is the real reason to come here. Everything is served in a wacky way. The menu doesn't tell you how, but I can give you the lowdown." He winks at me before pointing to the first item on the list. "This is served in a glow-in-the-dark skull."

"A glow-in-the-dark skull?" I repeat, making sure I've heard that right.

"Mm-hmm." He points to the next one. "This one comes in a serving vessel that looks like a red lantern, and the next one comes in a phoenix-shaped ceramic cup."

Maybe it's because I've already had a couple of drinks, but I'm overly amused by this. It might also be the fact that Brian is leaning close to me, and I feel like I'm in on some delightful secret.

He continues down the list. The next cocktail is called Electric Blue, and it contains blue curacao, among other things.

"It's served in a lightbulb," he says.

"How does that work?"

He shrugs. "Order it and see. It's hardly a unique idea. I came across lightbulb glasses both in Taiwan and New York before I saw them here. Alright, this next one comes in a small cauldron, with smoke brimming from it. Dry ice, of course. This one looks like it's served in a dragon's egg…"

He reaches the last item on the menu. Wild Beary has gin and berries, plus a couple of ingredients I don't understand, but it sounds tasty.

"How's that one served?" I ask.

"Oh, you have to order it and see."

I'm wary, but when our server comes around, I order it anyway, and Brian gets the Electric Blue.

The vibe in this place has changed since we arrived. I'm starting to feel like I'm not cool enough for it, but Brian fits right in.

Three women are seated at a high-top table near us. Another server brings over their drinks—two are of the glow-in-the-dark skull variety. The women immediately take out their phones and start snapping pictures.

"Here you are." Our server sets a glass bowl of ice in front of Brian. The lightbulb, full of blue liquid, is nestled in the ice, and the straw has yellow and white stripes. "And for you."

When the server sets my drink in front of me, all I can do is stare.

I'm not sure I've ever been more stunned in my life, not even when Brian bid twenty thousand for a date with me.

He's laughing at me now, and I don't blame him. Besides, it's a good-natured laugh.

The serving vessel is shaped like a grizzly bear's head. Its mouth, lined with sharp teeth, is open, displaying the ice and liquid inside.

Which, by itself, is already pretty fucking weird.

But the weirder part is that the grizzly's teeth are covered in red, like it just ate something bloody. Or a very large quantity of wild berries. I shit you not.

"The blood is edible, sir," the waiter says. "Raspberry and blackberry syrup."

"Uh, right. Thank you," I manage to say.

I can't stop staring at my drink. It's the strangest thing I've ever seen, yet disturbing as it is, I kind of love it? I want to put it in a story and make it a metaphor for…

I don't know what.

My alcohol-soaked brain is contemplating the meaning of being served a cocktail from the bloody mouth of a bear when there's a shriek. I snap my head to the right. One of the women at the nearby table has fainted, and a waiter manages to catch her before she hits the floor.

"She was looking in our direction," Brian says. "I think she saw the blood in your drink."

Once the woman has been revived, the server leads the group to another section in the lounge, far away from us.

My cocktail turns out to be much more delicious than it looks.

Next, I get the drink that comes in a dragon's egg, which seems excessively normal in comparison, though the taste is unusual and just as good as the previous one. Among the many ingredients is something called aquafaba, which Brian says is the liquid in which chickpeas have been cooked.

By this point, I'm rather drunk, and I find this information quite entertaining.

Yeah, I'm the kind of drunk who finds everything hilarious.

I'm also a touchy-feely drunk, even though I'm the opposite when I'm sober. I drape my arm over Brian and say, "This is the best night I've had in ages."

Is it because I particularly enjoy drinking from a bear's head?

This sets off a round of giggles.

However, Brian stiffened slightly when I put my arm around

him, so I start to back away, not wanting to make him uncomfortable.

"No," he says, "it's fine. I don't mind."

"You don't have to put up with it, though. I can keep my hands to myself."

I continue to shift away, but he puts his arm around my waist and pulls me back. It's kind of nice, sitting here like this.

With all the worrying about my writing and my apartment—as well as the gala and bachelor auction—I haven't been able to properly relax and have fun in a while. And sometimes having fun can be stressful, you know? All these decisions to make. I have a few friends, but we're terrible at figuring out what to do, which is why Spencer and I always end up at the same coffee shop.

Brian, however, doesn't seem to have that problem.

"You're okay." I try to punch him lightly in the shoulder to emphasize my point, but instead, I nearly knock over his cauldron.

"You're okay, too."

Then he gives me a look I can't decipher. My heart rate kicks up a notch, like I know something important is about to happen.

"I was thinking," he begins. "You want to be my roommate?"

I nearly spit out my sip of dragon's egg cocktail. "Your roommate?"

"Well, I have a room, and you need a place to stay. I'll figure out an acceptable amount for rent and run it by you tomorrow?"

He's the serious one now, which isn't how I expected the night to go.

"You want to live with me?" I ask.

"Why not? We get along, and to be honest, I'd like a roommate. I don't have a job, and I'm kind of lonely these days."

Really not the sort of thing I expected Brian Poon to say. I half think he's telling me this because he assumes I'm too drunk to remember, but I'm not. I mentally pin his words to my brain with a big wad of sticky tack.

Or a big…pin.

Then something occurs to me. "Is there space for me to work? Like, outside my bedroom?" I'd prefer if it wasn't like a dorm in university.

"The third bedroom is an office. I'm not in there much. I'll work around your schedule, and I won't be disruptive."

Somewhere inside my brain are skeptical thoughts, but I don't voice them. To be honest, I doubt I could string the words together now.

"Cedric?" he says.

"Yeah, I'll live with you."

He smiles widely. He seems absurdly happy about this, or maybe my brain is interpreting things incorrectly right now.

"Think about it overnight," he says. "Then you can come over to see the place."

I reach for my dragon's egg and sip the very last of it up the red straw.

"You're cut off," Brian says. "I'm gonna order some food to sober you up."

I perk up a bit, even though I've eaten more than enough food today.

Fifteen minutes later, a long rectangular plate with three char siu sliders is placed before us. I grab one and take a bite.

"Mmm. Fsljaiuipr," I say.

Or something like that.

Brian eats a slider and leaves the third one for me. We've had the same amount to drink tonight, but he seems no more than slightly tipsy.

I've always been a cheap drunk, though.

He gets us a cab and directs the driver to my apartment.

"You okay to get upstairs by yourself?" he asks when the car pulls up to my building.

"Yeah." I successfully open the car door. I'm feeling a little more clear-headed now. "Thank you for today."

"Anytime."

I stumble into my apartment, drink a bottle of water, and collapse on my bed.

~

The next morning, I wake up at nine, and one of my first thoughts is, *Brian is lonely*.

Those words I pinned to my brain. They're still there.

I don't feel too bad—not enough to warrant a painkiller. And I remember everything that happened yesterday.

Yeah, it was a good day.

I throw on some clothes, head to the kitchen, and make myself some coffee. My phone pings as I'm adding milk and sugar, and I can't help smiling when I see it's Brian.

You feeling okay this morning? he asks.

Yep, I'm good.

He sends me a figure for rent, and it's very reasonable. In fact, I think he's undercharging just a little. I expect he's aware of this. It's still far from cheap, but this is Toronto, and there would be many advantages to living with Brian, such as the location. It's farther from the college, but a long walk or short subway ride away, which is nice. I'd given up on finding anything reasonable downtown, until now.

Last month, I'd briefly considered getting a roommate, but I'd nixed the idea because I didn't know anyone who needed a roommate and wouldn't feel comfortable living with a stranger. Though I don't know Brian Poon well, surprisingly, I feel comfortable with the idea. Of course, I don't know what he'd be like to live with, but from the past couple of days, I have the sense he'd be a courteous roommate. If he were still a party animal, I don't think I could handle it. However, I could use a little more fun in my life, which I will balance with writing. Hopefully.

With any luck, a new space and a new routine will get me out of my rut.

I check the news on my phone as I sip my coffee, and then I nearly jump out of my chair when I realize what day it is.

Monday.

Mom and Po Po are going to show up any minute with two hundred dumplings.

My apartment isn't a dump, and some stuff is packed away in boxes—it was less stressful to pack than to look for a new apartment—but it still requires some tidying. It's not so much a question of stashing away things that will elicit disapproval, but things that'll elicit questions, although I'm sure they'll have no shortage of questions regardless.

By the time my phone rings, my apartment is looking pretty good.

"Buzz us in!" Po Po says.

Five minutes later, she and my mom are in my apartment, and I'm stuffing the dumplings into the freezer.

Yep, participating in the bachelor auction was worth it.

I make some tea for Mom and Po Po, and when we sit down at my small kitchen table, they look at me expectantly.

"What?" I ask.

"Your date!" Mom says.

"We want to know how it went." Po Po grabs my hand. "Was it okay?"

"It wasn't really a date, but yes, we hung out on Valentine's, and it was fine."

"Ah, 'fine,' this is such a boring word."

"We had dim sum, lobster, dessert, and drinks."

There's several seconds of silence.

"Aiyah!" Po Po smacks her hand on the table. "I made you two hundred dumplings, you owe me details."

"That wasn't part of the deal."

"It was implied! What if I die tomorrow? You will be at my funeral, crying, wishing you had told me about what you did on Valentine's Day."

"Somehow, I doubt that," Mom says.

I can't help thinking of last night's drinks. I don't even know how I'd describe those to my grandma, but I decide to try. Perhaps this detail will satisfy her.

"We went to a lounge with interesting cocktails. Brian drank one that came in a lightbulb."

"I do not understand," Po Po says. "Is this some weird back-alley bar where they are too cheap to pay for proper cups?"

"No, it's a rather fancy place." I pick up my phone and look for a photo. "Here. See?"

"You're sure that's not poisonous? It's bright blue!"

I also show her a picture of the dragon's egg cup but skip over the bear one because I fear that would raise too many questions.

She's more impressed when I show her pictures of the lobster.

"That looks tasty," she says. "Better than blue lightbulb drink."

"Well, I'm glad it went *fine*," Mom says. "Will you participate again next year?"

"I—"

"No!" Po Po interrupts. "I don't want you to still be single next February. I want you to find a *spouse* before I drop dead. You are the last one."

Yeah, yeah, I'm getting old. But even though I'm thirty-six, I feel like I've only recently started figuring things out.

"Don't worry," Po Po says. "I will not try to set you up with anyone—"

"I'm sure he's very thankful for that," Mom says.

"I will just bug you about it. Every week, I will come over and ask about your dating life." Po Po rests her chin in her hand and looks at me.

"Will you bring more dumplings?" I ask.

Mom swats me. "Stop trying to make more work for your poor grandmother. Hasn't she already made you enough?" She turns to Po Po. "I'm not driving you here every week."

"We'll see about that." Po Po sniffs.

"I'll only live here until the end of the month anyway," I say. "I have to move."

"What did you do wrong?" Mom demands.

"Are you too loud?" Po Po asks. "Playing bagpipes all day?"

"It was sold, and the new owner is moving in," I say, "but I have another place arranged."

"Give me a pen. What is your new address? I will be your first visitor."

"Let's give him a little space," Mom says. "I'm sure he'll tell us eventually."

I shoot her a grateful look.

"By the way," Po Po says, "I have been thinking of more story ideas. Instead of a grandma making marijuana dumplings, what if your book is about a *talking* dumpling? Could be like…post-post-modernism? Is this a thing?"

Mom stands up. "Alright, Ma. Time to go home and have a nap."

"But I was just getting started!"

After they leave, I stand in my kitchen contemplating talking edibles, cocktails served in bear heads, and how the hell I'll ever get another novel out of my brain.

[6]

BRIAN

"Ma asks about you every time I talk to her," Winnie says over the phone.

I slouch on my sofa and scrub a hand down my face. "What do you tell her?"

"I say you're doing well and bought a new place in…Yorkville? That's the area of Toronto you live in, right?"

"Yes."

"But I don't tell her a lot."

My sister wouldn't have much to tell our mother unless she started making shit up. It's not like Winnie knows a great deal about my life.

Winnie and I have never been super close—she's ten years older, and we didn't grow up together—but she's always doted on me as a younger brother. She and her husband live in the US.

I usually have words at the ready, but I have no idea what to say when she brings up our mother.

"I've got to go," I mumble. This isn't a lie. Cedric is coming over after he's finished teaching to see my place.

When I get off the phone, I barely have enough time to get a drink of water before the phone rings again and Cedric asks me to buzz him in.

All of a sudden, I'm nervous.

What if he doesn't like my condo?

It's somehow very important that he likes it.

I look around frantically, trying to see it through his eyes. Does he have the same taste in art as me? Will he like the glass wall sculpture in muted blues, for example?

But it's too late to change such things now.

I greet him at the door a few minutes later. He takes off his shoes and winter jacket, and he puts down his messenger bag in the front entrance.

"This is the living room." I gesture to the black sectional and the large TV. "Here's the bar. You're welcome to help yourself whenever you like."

He blushes slightly, perhaps remembering Sunday night.

I head to the kitchen. "Here's the, uh, espresso machine."

"You're showing me the important things. The alcohol and caffeine."

I flash him a smile. It's wobbly, though.

Why am I nervous?

"Here's the bathroom." I open the door so he can peek inside. "And the office. Lots of room for your stuff."

My office set-up is pretty minimalist. Just a sleek glass desk with a laptop.

I can tell he's going over things in his head, visualizing where his desk would go.

"This would be your room," I say as we move down the hall and I open another door. "It's currently set up as a guest bedroom, but I'll get rid of everything to make space for your stuff. Not a problem. By the way." I swallow. "You're free to have guests, of course, including of the overnight variety. Just give me a head's up."

"Um, I don't think you need to worry about me having

overnight guests in the near future." He's clearly uncomfortable talking about this.

I can't help feeling a bit relieved. Something about Cedric bringing people to his room and shutting the door... It bothers me, apparently, which I don't understand. This isn't like me.

But I don't let on that I'm anything but my ordinary self.

We head back to the living room and sit on the couch.

"So, what do you think?" I ask.

"It's great." He smiles at me.

"The only issue is that I don't have a second parking spot, so if you have a car—"

"I don't."

"Oh, and I have a cleaning lady who comes by on Thursday afternoons."

"I can pay you for half—"

I wave this off. "I'd be paying for it either way."

Hiring a cleaning lady once a week—and I pay her well—is nothing compared to all the upkeep my old house needed. Yes, I'm aware this makes me sound like a spoiled little rich kid.

"You'll move in?" I ask.

He nods.

I don't know why the prospect of having a roommate excites me this much, but it does.

My life is a far cry from what it was a year ago.

After Cedric leaves, I make myself a latte and think about my promise to Vince. I said I wouldn't "screw around" with his brother, and I still have no intention of doing so, though Cedric Fong is kinda my type. He's a little taller and broader than me, and he has a rather intense resting face, which always makes me wonder what's going on in his mind. But when you're talking to him, he's reasonably cheerful and easygoing, and I like that contrast. He's also got dark hair that refuses to behave, and I keep itching to run my hands through it.

Since he clearly isn't interested in me, I'm happy to have him live here. Plus, sleeping with a roommate seems like too much of a complication anyway.

But although I'm not breaking my promise to Vince, I'm not sure he'd see it that way.

~

"Ginny wants a goat for her birthday." Ted makes a face, as though this is the most horrifying idea ever.

To be fair, Ted is grumpy about a lot of things.

Michael, Ted's husband, cracks up. "I told her that farm animals aren't allowed in townhouses in Toronto. She said we could keep it in the backyard, and I said farm animals aren't allowed even in backyards. Then she pointed out that the old lady down the street has three chickens—"

"Ooh, she got you there," Kris says.

"—and I said chickens are a special exception. To which she stuck up her nose and replied that I should ask the mayor for a special exception for her goat. Apparently, the goat's name will be Wiggles, and he will be black with white spots." At this, Michael breaks out in laughter again.

We're at a bar. It's a little southwest of Yonge and Bloor, not far from where I live.

Ted and I met back in university, when he did things like study and attend class. Me? Not so much. But he was also a queer Asian guy, so we did have something in common. We were friendly, but not close.

A year ago, I ran into him at a restaurant, where he was having dinner with an attractive Black man, who turned out to be his husband. Michael apparently met Ted in university, too, but I didn't know him then. He works part-time as a physiotherapist and spends most of his time parenting their two kids, Ginny (five) and Eli (three). They live in the Beaches.

Kris Kim—petite, loud, bisexual—has been friends with them

for a while, and she lives around here, but not somewhere as hoity-toity as Yorkville.

This group is quite a bit different from the people I used to see on the weekends. Ted, Michael, and Kris just like hanging out at the bar and having a few drinks. Nothing fancy. It's a nice change.

"I am sooo going to show up at your house with a goat next weekend," Kris says to Ted.

"Where are you getting this goat?" I ask.

"Steal it from Riverdale Farm?"

"Well, since Michael isn't friends with the mayor"—I give him a look that says this is disappointing before turning to Ted—"why don't you sponsor a goat at an animal sanctuary?"

"Oooh, that's a good idea!" Kris says. "Much more practical than mine."

"That was my suggestion," Ted says, "but unfortunately, Michael had a bad experience as a child and won't let us do it."

"A bad experience with sponsoring a goat?" I ask.

"For my birthday when I was six," Michael says, "my aunt sponsored an iguana for me. I found the whole thing rather disappointing. I just got a certificate, nothing fun to play with, but my mother assured me we'd visit it at the zoo soon, and wouldn't that be exciting? But it never happened."

"Why not?" Kris asks.

"Because the iguana *died*."

Kris spits beer across the table, which makes her laugh even harder.

Ted's lips twitch.

"I'm serious!" Michael said. "We got a letter a few weeks later saying that unfortunately, my iguana had passed away. They offered me a different reptile instead, but I didn't want it. I felt guilty, like maybe I'd done something to cause the iguana to expire, so I barely ate until my mother figured out what was going on."

"Okay, I have a better idea," I say. "There's a goat and llama farm an hour out of the city."

"Are you suggesting goat yoga?" Kris asks.

"No, they have sessions for families where you get to, uh, cuddle and play with Nigerian Dwarf goats. They even have their own goat playground."

Frankly, this isn't my cup of tea. Goats are best observed from the safety of my home. On a screen. I can't imagine the mess and smell.

"How do you know about this?" Kris asks.

I shrug. I have a good memory for these sorts of things.

Michael punches my shoulder. "That's a great idea."

Ted looks less than thrilled, but I'm sure Michael will convince him.

I've met Ginny and Eli a few times. Ginny is a hurricane. I mean, she's great, but I'm glad she's someone else's kid. She accidentally—so she claims—dumped glitter on my head once, so I'm not sure if that means she loves me or hates me.

I swear I still find pieces of glitter on my skin.

"What's new with you, Brian?" Michael asks.

Oh, I bid twenty thousand dollars for a date with my crush's brother and got him drunk on weird cocktails. You know, normal things like that.

I take a sip of my drink. "Not much."

"No orgies in the back of private jets?" Kris asks.

"I never should have told you that story," I mutter.

To be honest, I like when they give me shit about stuff like this. It's all good-natured, and they don't take anything too seriously. We just goof off, nobody's trying to impress anyone. It's relaxing.

"I'm getting a roommate," I say.

"A roommate," Michael repeats. "Of the goat variety?"

"You think you're funnier than you actually are," Ted says.

"Isn't, like, having a roommate enough to revoke your rich-person card?" Kris asks.

"I thought I'd enjoy the company." And the fact that the rent money will cover the condo fees, more or less, is a help.

"I can understand that," Michael says.

Ted's face doesn't suggest such levels of understanding.

"He's just a *roommate*," I say. "Not a hook-up."

"Never said otherwise," Ted murmurs.

I see my mistake. My friends weren't suspicious before, but now they're suspicious because I felt the need to mention I'm not hooking up with Cedric.

I guess Vince's little speech has made me defensive.

"It's like this." I explain how I bid on Cedric at the bachelor auction, and how we spent Valentine's together. "And then I spontaneously suggested we live together."

Kris is just staring at me.

"He's Vince's brother," I add.

"Drama!" Michael says in a singsong voice, and Ted makes a show of covering his ears.

"Is he straight?" Kris asks.

I shake my head. "That's why I was allowed to bid on a date with him. But nothing's happening between us, trust me."

I don't let on that I'm slightly disappointed by this; I just calmly sip my beer.

When there's silence, I say, "Really, and it's not like I'm attracted to him just because he's Vince's brother."

"But you *are* attracted to him," Ted says.

"I'm attracted to lots of people. Whatever. It's not a problem for me. We're friends. Maybe I'll bring him around next time?"

"Definitely," Kris says.

At midnight, we pack it in. Once, this would have been ridiculously early for me, but I don't mind now.

When I get home, I slip off my boots, remove my second-favorite cashmere sweater, and think about the fact that in a couple of weeks, I'll no longer be coming home to an empty condo each night. I rather like the thought.

And as I get ready for bed, I wonder what Cedric will think of Ted, Michael, and Kris.

I also can't help wondering how he feels about goats.

[7]

CEDRIC

IT's the last Sunday in February. Moving day.

By mid-afternoon, I'm mostly moved in, and I take a look around my new bedroom. Bed, dresser, plus two bookshelves, which will stay in here rather than the office since there's more space. Right now, they're empty, but my boxes of books are sitting next to them.

I exit the bedroom and head to the bathroom. Except I'm not used to this place and I accidentally open the door to Brian's bedroom instead. His bed is a king, low to the ground, and I assume the sheets have a very high thread count. There's a pair of black bedside tables, and something about them seems quite sophisticated.

I puzzle over why that is and try to find the words to describe them. Perhaps it's partly because there's nothing on the surface except a single tiny cactus and a watch.

"Looking for something?"

I jump. Brian is standing right behind me.

"Sorry," I say. "I turned the wrong way. Still getting used to the layout."

We stand there in awkward silence. I feel like his eyes are boring into me.

"I like your bedside tables!" I blurt out.

Oh, God.

I don't usually make a fool of myself.

Brian crosses his arms over his chest and smirks. He's wearing dark jeans and a purple sweater. This is Casual Brian, and he still looks put together.

I can't help being curious. What's beneath all that?

And I don't mean that I want to get him naked. There's just something about him that fascinates me. Makes me wonder who exactly he is, beneath what he shows to the world.

I've had a hint of it, and I want more.

"Yeah, they're quality night tables," he says at last.

I finally make it to the office and glance around. It'll be nice to have an office that isn't just the corner of the living room.

"Alright," I say as I put on my coat by the door. "I've got everything moved in. Now I'll drive the extra furniture to my parents' house. Be back in a couple of hours, okay?"

How much should we inform each other of our plans? I haven't had a roommate in a while, and I feel a bit weird about it, even though I'm still confident this living situation is a good idea.

I drive the U-Haul north to my parents'. It was a nightmare driving it around downtown—maybe deciding to do this myself wasn't the best plan. But Brian, in his fancy jeans and sweater, helped me move the big items, and my mother will help at my parents' house. Dad will probably want to help, too, but since he had a heart attack several years back, I've tried my best to keep him from doing such things. Perhaps I should have asked my brothers to assist with the move, but it might have been weird for them to interact with Brian.

My mom and I are reasonably efficient, despite Po Po's attempts to distract us. Or, in her words, supervise.

"You don't need any of this?" Mom asks as we move my small couch to the basement.

"Not for now," I say, "but don't get rid of it, okay?"

"Is your new place so small that you don't even have room for a couch?"

I suddenly feel a little self-conscious about my lack of money.

Yes, I know I'm lucky. My parents paid for my education, including the MFA in the States, and I could ask them for money or live with them if I need to. Their financial security made it easier for me to pursue a writing career, and I don't have to worry about providing for them financially as they get older. I'm privileged.

But sometimes I feel like I don't belong in my family. I'm the only one who ever had artistic interests, who had zero interest in business.

"Cedric?" Mom says.

I consider not telling them about my new living situation, or lying about who my roommate is. Except it'll be hard to keep that up forever.

"Oh, I'm living with Brian Poon." I try to sound all casual. "He's got a spare room, and the location is good."

"You're living with Brian?"

Ahhh. When did my grandmother get so close to my ear?

I turn toward her. She's not actually that close. She's just really, really loud.

Po Po declares a "time-out" from moving, and we go upstairs to the kitchen for tea and egg tarts. I start sipping my tea while my mom and grandmother sit down and stare at me.

"What's going on?" Dad walks into the kitchen.

"He's living with Brian Poon!" Po Po exclaims.

"It's no big deal," I say. "When we were hanging out on Valentine's Day, I mentioned I needed a place to live—"

"You told him that before you told us?" Mom asks.

"I am not getting the whole story," Po Po says. "Did you fall in love on your first date? You did not say anything before, but is this what happened? You are boyfriends now?"

I shake my head.

"That is good. I would not approve. Not because he is a man, you understand, but because he's a party boy. But you are roommates, and I think he will be a bad influence." She clucks her tongue. "I told you, I do not trust him."

"I'm thirty-six, not sixteen," I say. "No need to worry about someone being a *bad influence* on me."

"But you want to write another novel, yes? How will you be able to write when he is doing Jell-O shots in the next room?"

"I don't think Brian would lower himself to Jell-O shots."

Po Po sniffs. "That's what you think."

"He has better taste."

"Fine, he will be doing non-Jell-O shots off people's stomachs in the living room! How can you work in such conditions?"

Mom takes my hand. "Are you living with Brian because you want a more exciting life to provide inspiration for your writing?"

"What? No."

"Am still convinced Brian Poon is after my dumplings," Po Po says. "He thinks if he lives with you, he will get dumplings, and then he will hide the marijuana in them and sell them for lots of money."

"Or he'll just eat them as is," Dad suggests.

"You see," Mom says, turning to me, "you don't need an exciting life to get lots of wild ideas for your work. Your grandmother has a boring life—"

"Who are you calling boring?" Po Po demands.

"—and she has lots of wild ideas. Just from watching TV and movies."

I'm starting to get a headache.

"Does Vince know you two are living together?" Mom asks.

"Not yet," I reply.

"They had a falling out last year, and I don't know why."

"Vince's lifestyle changed a lot, that's all."

And there was the whole issue of Brian's crush, which Vince revealed to me when I asked why he and Brian didn't see each other much anymore. Not that my brother was bothered by a man having a crush on him, but it did make things awkward between them.

The rest of my family doesn't know about that, though.

Fortunately, Mom seems to accept my explanation.

"If you're ever in any trouble," she says, "you call us and we'll pick you up, no questions asked, okay?"

I laugh. "No questions asked? Really?"

"She's lying," Po Po says. "I will ask questions."

"No, I mean it," Mom says. "I'll keep my mouth shut."

I nod. "I know you'll have my back if I need it, but you're acting like I'm a teenager, not a grown-ass man. I can take care of myself, and Brian really is a decent guy who isn't going to lead me down a dark path."

"Ah, you're in love with him," Po Po says.

"I'm not."

"That is what someone who is in love would say! I see it on the TV."

Sometimes you can't win, no matter what you say.

Half an hour later, my dad and I return the truck, and then he drives me to my new apartment. With only the two of us, the drive is mercifully quiet.

When I step inside the building, I feel a sense of excitement.

A new apartment. It feels like a fresh start.

[8]

BRIAN

THE DOOR to Cedric's room is open just enough for me to see him kneeling on the floor, putting books on his shelf.

I knock.

"Come in," he says.

"I'm gonna order something for dinner," I say. "What do you want?"

"Um. Whatever you like."

There's a moment of awkward silence, like there was after he accidentally wandered into my bedroom.

"I'm pretty easy," he continues, and I tell myself not to take that in a sexual way, but my brain does what it does. "You have good taste. I'm sure whatever you pick will be fine."

Now I feel extra pressure.

But he's right. I *do* have good taste. The problem is narrowing down all the possibilities.

An hour later, we're sitting at the dining room table, a platter of nigiri and sashimi in front of us. Next to it is a plate of maki.

"Wow," Cedric says. "I've never seen anything like this. It's almost too pretty to eat."

"Mosaic sushi."

"Will you laugh if I take a picture?"

I gesture toward the food. "Go ahead. I've already taken one and put it on Instagram."

The mosaic sushi has been rolled and cut very carefully. Each piece is a square. There's salmon in a diamond shape in the middle, and a quarter of a cucumber slice at each of the corners. A layer of white rice curves around the cucumber, followed by pink rice—not sure what's in that. When the nine square maki are all placed next to each other, it's like a set of tiles.

"Mmm," Cedric says after eating a piece of sashimi. "Very fresh."

There are tons of sushi restaurants in the city, and the quality of fish at this place is one of the best. I'm pleased he can appreciate that.

"What do I owe you for this?" he asks.

"My treat. It's your first night here. By the way, I try to eat at the dining room table or in the kitchen because I don't want to make a mess in the living room. Unless I'm having a party."

"And how often does that happen?"

"Not often."

After dinner, I offer him some bourbon. I can tell when I pull out the bottle that he knows it's expensive stuff. Not ridiculously expensive, but far from the cheapest thing at the LCBO.

I pour us each two fingers, and we sit on the couch in silence for a few minutes.

"So, what's your writing schedule?" I ask. "I'll stay out of here while you're working."

"Oh, I don't mean to kick you out of your home."

I wave this off. "I insist. You want to start writing again, and I want to make sure that happens."

He looks at me intently over the rim of his glass, and it causes an unfamiliar sensation in my stomach. It's as if he's trying to see into my brain.

I'm not used to people looking at me like this.

No, people look to me for a good time, for a laugh, for sex. That's who I am.

But sometimes it seems like Cedric takes me very seriously, even though I got him to drink from a fucking ceramic bear head, and I don't know what to do with that.

I drop my gaze and notice he's wearing flannel plaid pajama pants. They look cozy.

I kind of want to take them off…

Okay, I have sex on my brain. Nothing new. But it's different from how I usually feel attraction, and I don't know how to explain it.

"Brian?" he says. "Why are you so keen on making sure I start writing again?"

"You want to write, so I want you to write."

He continues to look at me in that strange way of his.

I can't stop myself from talking. "You have something you want to do with your life. I don't, but if I did…"

The truth is, I didn't particularly like Cedric's first novel. I read it because he's Vince's brother and I was curious. Although I could appreciate that he's very skilled at what he does, it just wasn't to my taste.

Not that I have any intention of telling him that.

Anyway, having him live with me has given me some sense of purpose, as weird as that sounds. I will be a great roommate, and I will get him writing again.

This isn't like me. I've always been trouble.

My mostly absent father was frequently exasperated with me. I wasn't who he wanted me to be—and that started decades before he learned I was queer. I wasn't terribly interested in school and goofed off a lot. I wasn't at all interested in his business. After a while, it became a game: how annoyed could I make my father? He just gave me money, told me not to cause him too much grief, and didn't expect anything of me.

But my father and brother are no longer part of my life, and partying has lost some of its luster now that it no longer pisses people off.

My mother's not like them, but she always wished I cared about pleasing my father. I think she would have been much happier if she'd married someone else.

I'm a chronic disappointment, but at the very least, I'm determined not to disappoint Cedric. It's more than that, though. I'm envious of how he knows what he wants to do, and so I won't let him fritter his time away. I figure I can do that much, and maybe his influence will also help me figure out what the fuck I should do with my own life.

Cedric is still quiet. He doesn't make me explain myself more than I already have.

"So," I say brightly, "when do you intend to write?"

"I usually just write when I feel like it, but I'm going to try setting a schedule and sticking to it, at least at the beginning. Monday, Tuesday, Wednesday, and Friday mornings. Say, eight thirty to eleven thirty."

"What about Thursday?"

"I teach on Thursday mornings, so until the semester is over, that's not an option."

"I'll be sure to be out of your hair the other days."

"As I said, you really don't have to…"

But I do. I have to show myself that I'm at least good for something. Even if that something is simply staying out of the way.

He has a sip of his drink, and I watch his Adam's apple as he swallows. And when he heads to his bedroom, I watch his ass in those flannel pajama pants as he walks away.

I can't help who I am.

When I go to my own bedroom, I recall Cedric poking his head in here earlier and saying something inane about my bedside tables, like he was super embarrassed to be caught looking in my room and wondering how my high thread-count sheets would feel against his skin.

I get ready for bed, but when I turn out my light, I don't feel as tired as I should. Instead, I keep picturing his intense gaze.

Maybe this roommate situation is going to be a little more complicated than I thought.

[9]

CEDRIC

I CRAWL out of bed at eight and get dressed.

I am going to write this morning.

The thought fills me with dread.

I claim to love writing, but I never seem to want to do it, and most of what I've written in the past several years has ended in frustration.

And not actually ended. I quit before the end.

I try to think positive thoughts as I open the door to my room and walk down the hall to the washroom. I don't know whether Brian will be up yet, but—

Wait. He must be up.

Because someone must be responsible for the delicious smell coming from the kitchen.

I'm still half-asleep, and it takes me a moment to process the scene in front of me. Brian Poon is taking a tray of cookies out of the oven?

Okay, this is totally not what I expected when I agreed to live with him.

"Good morning," he says as he turns off the oven. "Sleep well?"

"Uh, yeah."

"That's good. Help yourself to coffee." He gestures at the large French press in the center of the kitchen island. "Or I can make you something else." He motions to the espresso machine.

He's wearing chinos and a sweater, covered with a simple cream apron. Not a hair is out of place on his head. It's like some portrait of domestic bliss. Like I'm in an ad.

"Thanks." I grab one of the empty mugs he's set out and pour myself some coffee. I usually have two cups in the morning—my brain won't be fully functional until I have caffeine in me. "I didn't know you could bake."

"I've done it once or twice before."

"Cookies for breakfast?"

"Do you not like them?" He seems a touch…vulnerable.

I laugh awkwardly. "No, no, they look great. I'll just give them a moment to cool."

He shoots me a smile as he takes off his apron, seeming more like the suave guy I expected. "Who says you can't have cookies first thing in the morning? Besides, they have oatmeal, which I'm told is a very appropriate breakfast food, for people who care about things like being appropriate." He winks at me.

A few minutes later, I'm almost done my first cup of coffee, and he puts three cookies on a plate for me.

I take a bite and groan. "These are really good. It's been a long time since I've had cookies that are still warm from the oven."

I swear he's staring at my mouth.

No, that must be my imagination.

He looks at his phone. "It's almost eight thirty."

"Yeah, it is," I say reluctantly.

"Go on. Take your coffee and cookies into the office."

"I should help you clean up."

He waves this away. "It won't take long. Besides, I made these cookies specifically to keep you company while you write."

I'm not used to someone looking after me like this.

I focus on pouring more coffee. "You're not running a bed and breakfast. I'm just your roommate."

"What else am I going to do with my time? Let me do this for you."

I nod in thanks and retreat to the office, where I tell myself that I will not touch my phone until three hours are up.

I take out a new notebook, open it up, and write my name in it, as though I'm in school. Although I write my first drafts on the computer, I prefer brainstorming and planning on paper. I buy notebooks faster than I use them, however, and have quite the collection of blank ones.

At the top of the first page, I write, *Cocktail glass shaped like bear's head.*

I spend a few minutes wondering how I could fit that into a story, other than as an offhand mention to cause a laugh, before giving up.

I hear footsteps, and then the apartment door closes. Brian has left.

People who are not what they seem, I write.

There's nothing especially unique about that, but it's a decent starting point.

Various nebulous ideas float through my mind but nothing good enough to write down. Nothing that could lead to a novel.

This is too much pressure.

Brian is making me cookies and leaving the apartment so I can work. I feel like I can't let him down, and I'm not used to anyone being involved in my writing like this.

A horrifying thought occurs to me.

Will he want to read what I write? Will he ask me about it every day?

I notice a pile of books at the corner of my desk. Books I didn't put there. One is a copy of my novel, and it feels like it's taunting me.

I got a book published before I turned thirty, and I felt like I'd made it, and now...look at me. I can't do anything.

I pick up the books. Brian has placed a sticky note on the top one. *To read if you get stuck.* I study his neat, rather loopy handwriting. It's much nicer than mine, which is barely legible. Sometimes I write notes to myself and can't decipher them later.

The top book is a thriller, one I've never heard of.

Well, maybe I could read for a few minutes...

Next thing I know, it's eleven thirty.

Oops.

When I wake up on Tuesday morning and blearily leave my room, Brian is in the kitchen again. There are no freshly baked cookies, but once again, it smells good in here. The French press is full of coffee, and that's part of the aroma, but it's not all of it.

"I made granola," he says.

I eat some yogurt, granola, and banana with my first cup of coffee, and we talk a little.

I didn't see Brian much yesterday. I was preparing for my class in the afternoon, and he wasn't around at dinner—or after dinner. In fact, he was still out when I went to bed at midnight.

Is this what living with Brian Poon will be like?

Not that I have a problem with it. He's entitled to do whatever he likes.

I just enjoyed hanging out with him on Sunday, that's all. I guess I was hoping last night would be more of the same, but that's on me.

"Thanks." With my spoon, I gesture to the granola in my yogurt cup. "This is great."

He shrugs, as though it's no big deal.

I head to the office with my second cup of coffee, relieved he didn't ask about my writing.

Unfortunately, today is no better.

I can't think of anything I want to write about. I have an idea or two, but I know if I start writing, it'll end up like my previous attempts. Abandoned after the first few chapters.

Instead, I pick up the thriller and read.

And later that night, after I've taught my class and marked some papers and finished dinner, Brian still isn't home, and I open the book once more.

I stay up until two in the morning.

On Wednesday morning, I'm tired.

"Late night?" Brian murmurs as I walk into the kitchen.

"I was up reading one of the books you put on my desk," I grumble, not that I'm mad at him, of course. "It was very good."

"I made you muffins." He starts putting them on a rack to cool. "Carrot pineapple. It would help if you told me what you like so I know what to make."

"You don't need to bake for me every morning."

"Don't worry. It's not going to happen *every* morning."

I heard him come home at one last night, and he's up before me today, but unlike me, he looks well-rested. Is he one of those people who can function properly on a few hours of sleep?

Lucky bastard.

He serves me a muffin, and I pour myself some coffee. It tastes slightly different today.

"New beans?" I ask.

He nods and shoots me a smile.

I bite into my muffin. Carrot, chunks of pineapple, and walnuts. It's really good.

"You're an excellent baker," I tell him.

"I can follow recipes, and I have good equipment. That's all."

"I don't think I could follow a recipe before eight in the morning."

He laughs as though I'm funnier than I actually am.

Once again, I head into the office at eight thirty. I swear I'm not going to start reading another book today.

Sure enough, I don't.

I stand by the window and spend half an hour staring at the street, telling myself I'm people-watching for inspiration.

Then I sit at my desk and stare at the wall for twenty minutes.

I follow this up by staring at a blank notebook page for twenty minutes.

Any time I start really thinking about an idea, I lose interest. There's no way I could write three or four hundred pages.

After alternating between staring at the wall and the notebook for another twenty minutes, my mind drifts to Brian. Brian putting warm carrot pineapple muffins on a rack and smiling at me...

Yeah, that isn't going to help me write a novel.

I decide to just start writing, even if I have no idea what I'm doing. I write three disjointed pages about...nothing.

How the fuck am I being paid to teach a class on writing when I'm so bad at it myself?

True, it's not creative writing that I teach, but still.

I didn't used to be like this. I wrote stuff for my MFA and those three trunked novels in my mid-twenties. Not that they were *easy* to write, but most of the time, they didn't feel like pulling teeth.

And the fact that someone is spending three hours out of his own home every morning so I can have peace and quiet...well, that makes me feel even worse about using the time to stare at the wall.

At ten thirty, I consider getting up and doing some cleaning, but I'm supposed to sit here for three hours, so I will.

The last hour doesn't go any better.

~

Wednesday evening, I'm raiding Brian's liquor cabinet when the door opens. I'm not used to him being home in the evenings, and I feel guilty that he's caught me looking at his booze, even though he said I could help myself.

"How about I make you something?" he says.

"Uh, sure. If you like."

A few minutes later, he hands me a strong cocktail with ice. I'm not sure what it is, but it's good. He makes one for himself as well, then sits next to me on the couch.

I want to ask where he was today, where he usually goes in the evenings, but I don't.

Instead, he starts the conversation.

"How's the writing going?"

Oh, dear.

"It's not going," I say, "but the wall and I have gotten well-acquainted, since I spend so much time staring at it."

He laughs softly. There's something about his laugh, in the dim lighting—the lights in his fancy condo have lots of settings, and they're dim right now—that feels intimate. Like it's just the two of us, and the rest of the world doesn't matter.

Brian doesn't try to give me ideas or advice. He just says, "I'm sure you'll figure it out."

He speaks casually, as though his confidence in me is no big deal.

And yet, it kind of is.

Every day, he makes me coffee and breakfast, and he ensures I can spend three hours alone to write or stare at the wall. I was thinking of it as *pressure* before, but now I feel a strange sensation in my chest.

He...believes in me? Why?

We don't know each other that well. It's been years since my novel came out. I think my agent may have given up on me. My family is generally supportive, though maybe they feel obligated to support me.

But Brian certainly shouldn't feel obligated.

And him caring about someone else's work? It's not something I anticipated.

He's surprised me.

I study him. There's an elegance in the way he holds himself. He's wearing the same clothes as earlier, but with a patterned scarf wrapped around his neck. A scarf that would look ridiculous on me, but he can pull it off.

"Thank you," I say at last.

I don't write on Thursday because I'm teaching in the morning and preparing for next week's lectures in the afternoon.

Some people love teaching. Being in front of a class energizes them.

Alas, I'm not one of them.

I don't mind it, but to be honest, I wouldn't do it if I didn't need the money. The pay isn't great, but I prefer it to some of the other things I could do.

Friday morning, there's nothing baking, but Brian has made coffee and set out a plate of Wednesday's muffins and a bowl of fruit salad.

It's instinctive for me to tell him that this isn't necessary, I'm perfectly capable of making my own coffee and breakfast. But he knows that, and he keeps doing it.

I do appreciate it. When I step into the kitchen each morning and see him, warmth spreads through me. Even though the writing still isn't going anywhere, it's easy to get out of bed.

It just feels unbalanced because I'm not doing anything similar for him.

"This looks great," I say. "Thanks." I think he'd prefer hearing that than me telling him, repeatedly, not to go to all the effort.

And I suddenly get the sense that caring for someone is something Brian needs in his life but didn't have until now.

I take my coffee to the bedroom and open my notebook.

People who are not what they seem.

I read that line over again, and I have an idea.

At lunch, I decide to reward myself with my grandmother's dumplings. I ate half of them before I moved, but the other half I brought to my new apartment.

As I take them out of the freezer, I ponder the fact that I never worried about Brian eating my food. That's a sign of real trust.

Of course, if he knew how amazing these dumplings are, it might be a different matter.

No, I trust him, even though I had problems with a roommate stealing my food back in university.

When I have my steamed dumplings on a plate, plus a little dish of soy sauce and vinegar beside it, the door opens and Brian walks in, back from wherever he goes in the mornings. He enters the kitchen and stands beside me.

"Those look good," he says. "Where are they from?"

I'm instantly protective of my dumplings. I cover the plate with my hand, although what the purpose of this is, I'm not sure. He's already seen them, and he can smell them.

"Ah." A grin tugs at his mouth. "They're the dumplings your grandma made you to entice you to participate in the bachelor auction."

I try to distract him from the dumplings. "I wrote a few pages of a novel today."

Now he grins widely. "Yeah? That's great."

Luckily, he doesn't ask for details, since having to describe what I'm working on is one of my nightmares.

Really, it is.

For example, I once had a dream that I met Shakespeare on an elevator. I was in the middle of writing this amazing, amazing novel about dragon eggs. (It was a couple of days after I had that dragon egg cocktail with Brian.) I don't know what else the book was about; I just knew it was *amazing*. And I told Shakespeare that I was a writer—don't know what I was thinking—and he asked what I was currently writing.

Instead of answering, I melted into a rainbow-colored puddle.

It was very weird.

Anyway, unlike Shakespeare, Brian Poon doesn't ask such questions, but he does something nearly as bad.

"Can I try one?" He gestures at my plate, which I'm still covering.

I glare at him, and he seems to find this amusing.

"I made you muffins and granola and cookies this week," he says. "You're writing again. Don't you feel like being generous with me?" He knocks his hip against mine.

I am not amused, but he does have a point.

Brian has been good to me, and I've enjoyed having a room-mate so far.

"Okay," I concede. "You can have a dumpling."

"Really?"

"Shut up and eat it before I change my mind."

He grabs a pair of chopsticks, picks up a dumpling, and dips it in the sauce.

"How is it?" I ask.

He holds up a finger as he chews.

"A deeply religious experience," he says at last.

"Told you they're good."

He reaches for the last dumpling. I think he's just kidding around, he wouldn't actually eat a dumpling that I didn't give him permission to eat—the horror!—but I snatch it with my chopsticks just in case, and he laughs.

I'm about to rinse off my dishes when my grandmother calls.

"Hi, Po Po," I say.

"I have a new idea for you!"

"A talking bowl of rice rather than a talking dumpling?"

"Don't be ridiculous! A bowl of rice would never talk."

Yet a dumpling would? I don't ask for clarification.

"This time it is just a single word," she says. "A new word I learned from the TV today. I think it will be inspiring for you."

"Okay," I say, "let's hear it."

"Pyromania."

"Pyromania?"

"You do not know what it means?"

"I know what pyromania is." I glance up at Brian, who's laughing, and give him a mock glare. "But I don't know how this is supposed to inspire me."

"Aiyah! Someone who starts fires all the time—isn't this a great idea for a book?"

"It's not my cup of tea. And I've already started writing something."

"Ah, that is good! Which of my ideas inspired you? Is it the grandmother who puts marijuana in her dumplings to pay for her grandson's med school tuition?"

"Uh, no—"

"You know, it's very weird they're called 'edibles.' All brownies are edible, not just the ones with marijuana."

"Mm-hmm."

"Am I wrong?"

"Look, Po Po, I don't have time for this deep philosophical discussion right now—"

"You should always have time for your po po. I am your last grandparent. I could drop dead any minute!"

"—but I'm coming over for dinner on Sunday, okay? I'll see you soon."

"Hmph. Okay. See you then."

I end the call. Brian is snickering.

"You want to go out tonight?" he asks. "To celebrate that you're writing again?"

"It's too soon to celebrate, but we can go out for dinner, sure."

When he smiles, it brings me just as much pleasure as those delicious dumplings.

[10]

BRIAN

I'M RATHER ENJOYING my new life.

I know I don't *have* to wake up before Cedric and make him breakfast every day, but it gives structure and just a little bit of meaning to my week.

Once he's ensconced in the office, I head out. I go for long walks and try new coffee shops. When I sit down with my latte, flat white, or similar—I'm always trying different things—I take out a small notebook and pen from my pocket.

On the first page of the notebook, I've written, *Things I could do with my life.* I've underlined it four times.

Unfortunately, that's as far as I've gotten.

I'm not particularly good at anything, as my father never failed to remind me. My mother never put it like that. She'd just tell me that I needed to do a better job at applying myself and committing to something.

I'm pretty terrible at commitment, though.

I used to be content with just having fun, but it's not the same now. Getting up in the morning and making someone breakfast is at least something.

But I need more than that.

Today, I'm sipping a matcha latte at Harbord Coffee Bar. I turn to the second page in my notebook, deciding it's time for a new list: *Things I enjoy.*

Well, this is a little easier.

Dining out

Sex

Hmm.

After puzzling over the list for a little longer, I add a few more items.

Nice clothes

People

Drinking

Baking

I stare at the last one for a few minutes.

I've enjoyed baking recently, and I seem to be reasonably good at it. I only have my own opinions—possibly biased—and Cedric's to go on, but I'd know if I were terrible at it.

Though I can't say I'm interested in any kind of hardcore baking. I've no desire to spend vast amounts of time in the kitchen.

Is it just because I'm lazy?

"Brian!" Lucy, one of the baristas, sits down across from me. "How's the matcha latte?"

"Delicious."

"I got you something." She sets down a slice of roll cake on a plate. It's not quite as perfect as their normal fare, which is presumably why I'm being given it for free.

"You're a sweetheart," I tell her.

"It's matcha and red bean."

I have a bite. Although the appearance of the roll cake may have been compromised slightly, the taste hasn't.

I make an exaggerated grimace.

Her mouth pops open in an "O," and she reaches for the plate. "I'm *so* sorry—"

"Aw, give it back, I was messing with you."

She gives me a light-hearted glare.

"How's school going?" I ask. Lucy is doing her degree part-time.

We talk for a few minutes, and then she goes to help a big group that just came in. I return to drinking my latte and making my list...or not making it. Instead, I'm thinking about what else I could bake for Cedric. Should I try my hand at roll cakes? Biscotti?

Focus, Brian.

After half an hour of thinking about my future, I'm thoroughly discouraged. I leave the coffee shop, waving at Lucy on the way out, and head home.

Cedric is in the kitchen, eating ramen for lunch.

"What's wrong?" I ask.

We've been living together for almost two weeks, and I've become familiar with his expressions.

This is not a happy one.

"I hit a wall at the fifth chapter again," he says.

"I'm sure you'll figure it out."

He shakes his head. "This is just like all the other books I've started in the past few years and never finished."

"You know what you need? A muse. All those famous dead white dudes...didn't a lot of them have muses? Or was that just visual artists?"

"Are you offering?"

I tamp down my disappointment that he doesn't say this in a flirty way. He just seems confused by the whole idea.

But I do like the thought of being part of someone's creative process, and I actually think I'd make a good muse. I mean, it doesn't involve much aside from being supportive and looking pretty, right?

Though I kind of want something that's…my own.

I leave this muse idea behind. Cedric needs cheering up.

"Alright, scratch that," I say. "You need to take your mind off things. I'm thinking you should get laid…or drunk. One of the two."

As soon as I say the words, my skin feels itchy and uncomfortable. I don't usually feel this way when I talk about sex; it's something I do easily, but with him…

God, what's wrong with me?

He smiles as he slurps his ramen. "Sounds good. Where should we go?"

Since he doesn't offer any suggestions, I say, "Don't worry, I always have a few ideas."

After dinner, I take Cedric to a little bar just off Queen Street, one of those places that's hard to stumble upon if you don't know it's there, because it's so unassuming on the outside. But inside, it's intimate and classy. There are candles flickering on the bar.

The bartender's lips twitch when I approach, which is a big smile for him.

"Cedric, this is Naoki." I gesture to the bartender, who's dressed in black and has a low ponytail. "He's one of the best bartenders in Toronto."

Naoki doesn't object; he knows he's very good. I used to hire him to work at my parties, and he's not cheap.

"Cedric is my roommate," I explain. "I told you that I got a roommate, didn't I?"

I often come here on Tuesday nights. Not this past Tuesday, but I came last week, a couple of days after Cedric moved in. Tuesday nights are quiet here, and Naoki and I can chat.

And by that, I mean I talk and he puts up with me.

We've fucked a couple of times, too, back in the days before he got a boyfriend.

Pity about that.

Not that I'm looking for anyone for me tonight. Tonight is for Cedric.

"What would you like to drink? There's no menu here, other than the specials." I point to the blackboard. "You just tell him what kind of ingredients you like, and he'll make you something."

Cedric appears overwhelmed by the possibilities.

He's wearing gray pants and a black dress shirt today. Nothing fancy—Cedric isn't a snazzy dresser—but he looks good in his basic wardrobe.

"How about that drink with bourbon you made for me last week?" I say to Naoki. "One for each of us."

Naoki knows exactly what I mean. He has a great memory.

It's not long before he places our drinks in front of us.

"No lightbulbs or dragon eggs," I say to Cedric. "Just regular boring glasses." I lift up my glass and clink it against his, and then we both have a sip.

"Mmm," Cedric says. "Is there thyme in this?"

Naoki nods. I think he's impressed. The thyme is pretty subtle, but it adds a certain je ne sais quoi to the drink.

I don't like the way Naoki is looking at Cedric. I guess it's because I feel a little protective of Cedric. Because he's Vince's brother and my roommate?

Yes, that must be it.

I also don't like the way Cedric is now watching Naoki as he prepares drinks for another group. Is he interested in Naoki, or does he just enjoy watching someone who's good at their work?

I turn away and notice a familiar person waving at me from across the room. Ooh, it's Elsie. She's dyed her hair purple.

"Do you know people everywhere you go?" Cedric asks. He must not have been paying as close attention to Naoki as I thought.

I suppress a smile. "I guess? Nothing better to do with my life, you know."

Cedric looks like he's about to object, but then he sips his cocktail. I want to ask more about his writing, but I told him tonight was to forget, so I keep my mouth shut, which is difficult for me.

We're almost done our second drinks when Cedric gets a little handsy. He's not drunk, but he's definitely feeling the alcohol, and I'm not gonna lie, I enjoy slightly-tipsy Cedric. Me—I'm still sober. I have a good tolerance, even if I'm smaller than he is.

And when I say Cedric is "handsy," I mean he's occasionally touching me on the shoulder and putting his arm around me. Nothing more than that.

Naoki looks up and arches an *is-that-the-way-it-is?* eyebrow.

I just shrug with a smile.

Yeah, I'm rather enjoying Cedric's attention.

Elsie comes over a few minutes later and kisses me on the cheek. "Brian! I haven't seen you in ages."

"You have to come here on Tuesdays," I say.

She makes a face. "I'm too busy on Tuesdays."

"With work? Or your new woman?"

She blushes. "You have to introduce me to your boyfriend!"

At this, Cedric seems to realize that his arm is around my shoulder, and he drops it.

"No, no!" she says. "Nobody's going to say anything, not here."

"It's just," Cedric begins. "We're not..."

Ugh, what is happening to me? Did Naoki put some kind of special ingredient in this drink? Usually whenever someone makes a comment about me having a significant other, I inwardly freak out and outwardly laugh it off, but now I'm disappointed Cedric is immediately denying it, and I miss his touch more than I ought to.

"We're roommates," he says.

"We are," I say, jumping in because I don't want Cedric to feel uncomfortable. "It's not like I need three bedrooms to myself, and you know me. I'm social. Nice to have the company."

Elsie seems to accept this explanation.

"I like the color of your drink," I say. "It matches your hair."

"I know! That's what I asked for. A drink that matches my hair. Naoki, as always, performed a miracle." She holds out her phone. "Can you take a picture?"

I nod.

"Brian takes the best photos," she tells Cedric. "He has a great eye."

"She's not lying," I say. "I do. Love the hair, by the way."

A few minutes later, Elsie returns to the group of women she came in with, and I have Cedric all to myself again. I don't know why that thrills me, but it does.

He makes me a little mixed up. I'm going to blame it on the fact that he's Vince's brother and I've sworn to behave myself.

I stare at him as he walks to the washroom.

Naoki's lips twitch. "You want him but you can't have him."

"Shut up," I mutter.

"It's a new experience for you?"

I give him the stink eye.

When Cedric returns, he asks for a drink "with gin and citrus but not too sweet"—he seems to like gin—and Naoki makes him something, as well as a drink for me.

Close to midnight, Cedric says he wants to head out, and we grab a cab back to our place.

Our place. I kinda like that.

"Thanks," he says. "That was fun."

"You were just sitting there quietly and drinking."

"Still. It was good to get out."

"You were practically brooding."

"Was not!"

There's something about his outrage that's particularly adorable.

"You want to go out tomorrow, too?" I ask. "My friends are having beers."

I'm more pleased than I should be when he says, "Sounds good."

Yep, taking care of Ceric Fong and getting him out to have fun is now a big part of my life, and I'm not complaining.

[11]

CEDRIC

"So, you're writing again?" Spencer asks.

I pour more sugar into my coffee and stir, just for something to do as I avoid answering his question. We're at Fueled on Wellesley, which is where we almost always meet up because we're creative like that. It's also where we had our first date.

My friendship with Spencer is the one good thing that came out of my ill-fated attempts at using dating apps last year.

My past relationships were all with people I knew well first. The idea of looking at a picture and swiping left or right—I wasn't keen on the idea, but I figured it was worth a try. I went on a few lackluster dates.

But then one app suggested Spencer—white, curly brown hair, twenty-nine, located in downtown Toronto—to me, perhaps because we're both writers. And I thought, *Sure, why not?*

We went on a few dates. We talked, we got along. He asked if I wanted to go back to his place, and I said no, but I thought I might want that eventually. It seemed more promising than the other people I'd met through apps.

And then…well, he experienced love at first sight.

With a different guy.

At a different coffee shop.

They're still together, and it seems to be going well. And I can't say I'm unhappy about how things turned out. Spencer and I would have eventually discovered we were incompatible anyway.

But as friends? We're good.

He writes queer space opera, which he self-publishes with modest success, and works part-time at a bookstore in the Village. He's one of those annoying writers who manage to write a couple of thousand words every day and never seem to get writer's block.

"I, um." I sip my coffee. "No, I got stuck."

"Shit, I'm sorry." He pauses then shoots me a good-natured grin. "You want me to offer you advice?"

I laugh.

Many months ago, he asked me the same question, I say yes, and he proceeded to give me the worst advice I've ever heard.

Bad advice for *me*, I mean. Clearly, it's working okay for him. We might both be writers, but our brains work very, very differently.

So, this is an ongoing joke we've had ever since.

We talk about the shows we're watching, and then he stands up and says, "Be right back."

I pull out my phone and go to Brian's Instagram page. I've taken to looking at it once a day—okay, several times a day. He posts regularly, and it gives me some idea of where he goes when he's not home. Elsie's right: he does take nice pictures.

Seriously, I've never seen such a pretty picture of fried rice before.

When Spencer sits back down across from me, I quickly put my phone away, and he raises an eyebrow.

"What?" I say, perhaps a little harshly.

"Whatcha doing there, Cedric?" he asks in a singsong voice,

tapping his black nails on the arm of the chair. "A little flirty texting?"

"No. Definitely not." Why do I sound guilty? I'm not guilty.

"Making big plans for tonight?"

"Just going out with my new roommate and some of his friends."

"Didn't you go out last night?"

"I can go out two nights in a row."

"That's true," he admits, "but I don't remember the last time it happened."

He does have a point.

This is certainly more than my average amount of socializing.

"By the way," Michael says to Brian, "we took Ginny to the goat farm last weekend, and she loved it. She'd been so excited about going all week, and I was convinced it could never live up to her expectations, but it did."

"Who's Ginny?" I ask, sipping my beer.

I'm not a big beer fan, but if I'm hanging out somewhere for several hours, it's not a bad thing to drink. I can make it last, and I drink it so slowly that it never gets me drunk. And after last night, I figure I can take it easy tonight. Naoki sure makes strong cocktails, but damn, they were good.

"Our five-year-old daughter." Michael pulls out his phone and shows us a photo of a little Black girl, flanked by two goats. "She wanted a goat for her birthday, which, for obvious reasons, wasn't possible, and Brian suggested Goat's Haven."

"You're giving me too much credit," Brian says. "I vaguely remembered that such a place existed, and you had to Google it."

"But it was easy to Google. And you were right. She loved it."

I like this little group. It's just Michael and Ted (married) and an Asian woman with spiky hair whose name, I believe, is Kris.

I'm not sure I heard it right, and now I'm too embarrassed to ask.

I don't have as many queer friends as Brian does—Spencer is the only one I see somewhat regularly—and this is fun. It reminds me a bit of my group of friends from high school. There were five of us, and only one person was out at the time, but now we're all out. Funny how we found each other, even back then. Sadly, most of them don't live in Toronto now, and I don't see them much anymore.

I manage another sip of my beer. "Yeah, Brian is good at that sort of thing."

Ted nods at Michael, and apparently Michael knows exactly what this is about.

"Right," Michael says, turning to Brian. "I almost forgot. I told Ginny it was your idea, and she drew you a picture." He reaches into his bag and pulls out a child's crayon drawing. It's captioned with a single word: *GOATS*. The "S" is backward.

I study the drawing. There are two four-legged animals which look vaguely like horses, but I assume they're supposed to be goats. Next to the goats is a stick figure with a big head and a big frown.

"That's you," Michael explains to Brian.

"She got my hair wrong," Brian pats his head.

"Yeah, yours isn't as green as in the picture."

I point at the stick figure. "Why is Brian frowning?"

"Ah," Michael says. "Ginny explained that 'Uncle Brian is very sad because he didn't get to go to the goat farm with us.' She told me to invite you next time."

"Next time?" Brian croaks. "Has she convinced you to go there on a weekly basis?"

"She said she'd settle for monthly," Ted tells him.

"She also said to tell you"—Michael looks like he's holding back laughter—"that she will give you glitter. This is supposed to entice you to come."

"Glitter is fine in moderation," Brian says, "but—"

"Ginny doesn't know the meaning of moderation. I'm aware. Not that I mind the endless pictures of goats with glitter. They're lots of fun."

"They are," Kris agrees, then turns her attention to me. "So, what do you do, Cedric?"

This shouldn't feel like a loaded question, but it does.

"He's a writer," Brian says while I'm still pondering how to reply.

"That's cool," Kris says. "What do you write? Plays? Short stories? Listicles? Technical documentation?"

"Um, I have a novel," I mumble. "It was published several years ago."

"I'm going to look it up." Kris pulls out her phone. "What's your last name again?"

"Fong, right?" Ted says.

Well, this is horrifying.

"Oh wow," Kris says. "Looks like it was kind of popular. Have you read it, Brian?"

"Uh, yeah."

I snap my head toward him.

"What's with the look?" he asks.

Michael slaps the table. "I bet Cedric's debating if he can still live with you."

"There's some truth to that," I say, which makes Michael and Kris laugh.

"Has your family read it?" Kris inquires.

"My dad, my mom, my grandma, and my older brother read it. Although I'm not sure my grandmother read the whole thing—reading a novel in English is difficult for her—but she read the sex scene."

Everyone's laughing in a way that makes me feel like I belong, and it's nice, even if the memory makes me shudder.

"How did she manage to read only the sex scene?" Michael asks.

"When I gave a copy to my family, I marked off the section they weren't allowed to read with sticky notes. Of course, my grandma went right for that part, then insisted on having a very, very long conversation with me about it."

"I really wish I'd been there," Brian says.

"I'm very glad you weren't," I mutter, and everyone laughs again.

"Are you working on something new?" Kris asks.

I try not to stiffen, but I do.

"Sorry, sorry," she says. "Is that one of those questions I'm not supposed to ask?"

One thing I appreciate about Brian's friends is that they don't seem like the type to get in your face about stuff you don't want to discuss.

The conversation turns to Eli's new fascination with unicorns. Apparently, Ginny's younger brother is almost as obsessed with unicorns as she is with goats. Ted admits to being a little disturbed that Eli said he'd get a unicorn tattoo when he's really big and old. Which, to Eli, is six or seven.

When Brian and I leave, I'm in a good mood. We're not far from home, so we walk. It's a Saturday night, and there are a decent number of people out and about.

"Brian," I say suddenly, "do you want kids?" After the conversation about Ginny and Eli, that's one of the things on my mind.

He shoves his hands into the pockets of his posh wool coat. "Nope, never wanted kids. Probably in part because my father's a piece of shit—"

"I'm sorry."

"But even if I had a happier family life, I suspect I'd feel the same."

"I wasn't sure what I wanted," I say, "but then Julian and Courtney had Evie, and I saw what their lives were like. Call me selfish, but it's not my thing. And I'm never sure how to interact with her. I'm a little better now that she's started talking, but I'm not a natural with kids. Not like Vince."

I immediately regret mentioning my brother.

There's a moment of awkwardness while we cross the street, and then Brian says, "I like other people's kids. I like handing them over to someone else when they need a diaper change or a clean outfit. Some people say they don't particularly love kids but always wanted to be a parent because having their own kids would be different. But I'm the opposite."

"Same."

He smiles at me before looking ahead again, and I feel a strange bond between us, just agreeing on this one little thing.

But it's not such a little thing, if you're in a relationship. It's one of the reasons Spencer and I never would have worked out, but Brian…

Am I really thinking about being in a relationship with Brian Poon?

No. I shake my head and look over at him, just as wet snow starts to fall. White specks on his elegant dark coat. I wonder what he's thinking about—it's certainly not the same thing as what's on my mind.

"In fact," Brian says, "I'm so sure I don't want kids that I had a vasectomy."

I nearly bark out a laugh, even though that's not the appropriate reaction. It's just not what I was expecting him to say, even though it's on topic.

"It's better this way," he continues. "You know, since I screw around a lot."

"Did it hurt?"

"I've had worse."

When we get home, it's after midnight, but I still don't want to go to sleep. I change into pajama pants and a T-shirt then make a cup of rooibos.

Brian is sitting on the armchair in the living room, a small glass of liquor in his hand.

I take a seat on the couch.

"Is that rooibos?" he asks, making a face.

"Don't insult my tea."

He chuckles.

I nod at his drink. "You didn't drink much beer at the bar tonight. In fact, you nursed a single pint the whole time."

"You noticed that, did you?"

It feels like he's studying me intently. It's not exactly uncomfortable, just…weird.

He leans closer. "I'll let you in on a little secret."

I'm strangely excited by this whole secret business.

"I don't like beer," he says. "Yes, I could have gotten something that wasn't beer—"

"But the options weren't up to your expensive tastes?"

He smiles. "You know me well."

"I don't much like beer either, though it's more because of the effect it has on me, rather than the taste. Beer makes me sleepy."

"You don't seem sleepy now."

"Like you, I only drank a pint."

"I noticed."

It's very quiet for a moment.

I didn't know Brian well before we moved in together; I knew him mainly by reputation and from the stories my brother told. This quieter, slightly pensive and broody side of Brian isn't something I heard about.

Suddenly, I wonder if he's brooding about Vince, and I don't like the idea.

"Ted, Michael, and Kris aren't the sort of friends I expected you to have," I say.

"Because they're pretty chill and down-to-earth?" he says. "They drink cheap beer?"

"Do they know you don't like beer?"

"Nah. They'd tease me."

"They would, but they'd drop it if they could tell it bothered you."

"I don't want them to plan their nights out around my tastes. It's not like I don't go out enough. The occasional night of beer won't hurt me." He shudders in an exaggerated fashion.

There's something that's been on my mind all night. It's not the sort of thing I'd usually ask about—in fact, I'd do anything to avoid the topic—but I can't seem to help it with him. Maybe because he's been so dedicated to making sure I have my writing time.

"You read my book," I say. "What did you think of it?"

"It's well-written. You're very talented."

I smile slightly, however… "That's a bit of a non-answer."

"I mean it. You're good at what you do."

"But…"

"You really want to push this." He sighs. "It wasn't to my tastes, that's all. Doesn't mean there's anything wrong with it."

"What do you mean by 'not to your tastes'?"

"It's pretty straight and white, for starters, and there's not much action. But like I said, that doesn't mean there's anything wrong with it."

"There was a Chinese lady," I say defensively. "Mrs. Fu."

"True. She didn't appear on the page much."

"Why are you so keen on me writing if you don't like what I write?"

"I can be supportive without being a huge fan, and I want to be supportive." He has a big swallow of his drink and winces, as though it really burned on the way down. "But I can't help wondering if you keep getting stuck because of *what* you're trying to write. I assume it's similar to your first book?"

"Yeah." I study the liquid in my glass.

"Don't listen to me. You know I don't know anything about anything."

"What are you talking about? You know lots of things about lots of things."

He chuckles and looks away from me. "Fine. Think that if you like."

I'm silent for a minute before I say, "Back when I was in grad school, I wrote a story. We had to share them with small groups in the class, and two people asked me why the main character was Asian. They said it didn't affect the story at all, so why should he be Asian?"

"As if white is the default. You don't believe that shit, do you?"

"No, they're obviously wrong, but something can be wrong and still be what a lot of people believe. Sometimes I feel like if I want to write about Asian people in Canada, it should be a sad immigrant saga."

He hesitates, and I lean forward, as if whatever he's going to say next is very important.

"Why can't you write about a bi Asian guy?" he asks.

I laugh. "I don't want to write a story about myself."

"It won't be. I mean, maybe he has a fabulous roommate, too, but he fights crime or something like that. As far as I know, that's something you don't do."

I shake my head. "That's nothing like the stuff I've written before. It wouldn't *fit*."

"Maybe the stuff you usually write doesn't fit with who you are, and that's the problem?"

It's painful when people try to discuss my book, and here Brian is, saying I'm talented but should write something else. Attacking the decisions I've made for the past decade. Decisions that aren't simply because of a few things people said to me in grad school, even if he may assume that.

"You don't get it," I say.

"I know I don't get it. I know I shouldn't have said anything, but…"

Now I feel the need to reassure him, to get back to the way we usually are together. If I want to keep living here, it's important we remain on good terms.

"My grandma keeps trying to give me ideas," I say. "Like, a talking dumpling. Maybe it could talk to that bear cocktail glass, I dunno."

When Brian laughs, it warms my heart more than it should, so I keep going.

"She also told me to write a book about a grandma who adds cannabis to her dumplings and sells them to put her grandson through med school."

"Not gonna lie, that sounds awesome," he says. "Or maybe you could write science fiction. This grandmother could accidentally find her way onto a spaceship and it blasts off before anyone finds out she's there."

"How does one accidentally get onto a spaceship without someone noticing?"

"You're the writer."

I sigh. "The hard part is turning an idea into a whole book."

"I could never do it. But I think 'Po Po Blasts into Space' is a good start."

"It sounds like a children's book."

"Well, you could write children's books, though I was thinking a long, epic journey for adults. How many books have you read that describe aliens from the point of view of a grandmother?"

"I rarely read books about space."

"You could always start."

"Science fiction isn't really my thing." It works for Spencer, but not for me.

"I'm just saying." Brian finishes his drink and stands up. "I'm off to bed."

I nearly tell him to pour himself another drink and keep me company.

I don't, though.

He heads to his bedroom, and I stay in the living room with my rooibos tea.

~

Sunday, I do some laundry and mark some papers, and then I visit my family for dinner. I only see Brian briefly.

Monday morning, he's in the kitchen when I get up, and the French press is on the kitchen island. He pops a warm blueberry orange muffin onto my plate as soon as I sit down. Last time he made these, I told him they were my favorite of everything he'd baked so far.

I don't think it's a coincidence that he made my favorite today.

"Good morning." He pours us each a mug of coffee.

"Good morning," I say.

"I want to apologize for Saturday. I shouldn't have said what I did about your writing."

"I kind of pushed you to admit you didn't like my book."

"Like I told you, I don't know anything about anything."

It bothers me that he's said this yet again, because it's demonstrably not true. "You know how to make delicious blueberry orange muffins."

As soon as I speak, I wish I'd said something more profound. But sometimes, I'm not good with words.

I know, I know, I'm a writer. I should be good with words. Alas…

"It's fine," I say. "We're cool. You always make sure I have quiet writing time, and I really appreciate that."

I head to the office at precisely eight thirty and stare at the blank pages in my notebook.

On Saturday night, Brian's words kept me up. They made me a little angry, although it's impossible for me to truly be angry at Brian.

I can't write about some Asian guy and his fabulous room-mate, even if they solve crimes.

Solving crimes isn't the sort of thing I write.

And I definitely have no interest in writing science fiction.

I know he meant well, but *ugh*.

After thirty unproductive minutes, I pick up the books that Brian put on my desk. There is, indeed, one about space. Another is a cozy mystery about the residents of a retirement home.

I like cozy mysteries, so I read a couple of chapters, but even though I'm enjoying it, my mind keeps straying.

Mostly I read literary fiction, and I never enjoy lit fic as much as this, but I keep saying that's what I like to read and write. This book feels like a guilty pleasure.

Perhaps I'm a snob.

Perhaps I *should* write something completely different.

As I read about this extremely white retirement residence, I can't help thinking that someone like my grandmother would be a more entertaining character.

What if I really did write about an Asian grandmother who put cannabis in her dumplings, then discovered a dead body in the course of delivering them?

I start doing research and immediately locate a recipe for cannabis-infused dumplings.

[12]

BRIAN

It's Friday evening, and Cedric is in our home office with the door closed.

This is unusual. He normally only closes the door when he's writing, not when he's working on his course. And he normally only writes in the mornings.

I got home more than three hours ago, and he's been in there the whole time.

I knock on the door.

"Come in," he says absently.

I open the office door, and he continues typing for a few seconds before looking at me.

"Have you eaten dinner?" I ask. "It's nine o'clock."

"Oh, shit. Really?" He starts to stand.

"No, you stay there. I'll make you something. Your grand-mother's dumplings?"

For some reason, this makes him laugh. "Sounds good. You can eat some, too."

I look at him in surprise. He's really going to let me eat his prized dumplings?

"Is the writing going well?" I ask cautiously. "Is that why you forgot to eat?"

He's smiling. "I'm on chapter six. I haven't gotten this far on a book in years."

"Did I piss you off so much on Saturday night that it lit a fire under your ass?"

"No, you inspired me. I won't tell you what it's about yet, but it isn't a demisexual Asian dude solving crimes with his roommate."

He just described himself with a word I've never heard him use before, but he doesn't seem to be aware of what he's said.

"I've written five thousand words today," he continues. "I'm afraid if I stop, I'll lose my momentum."

"Then don't stop. I'll steam the dumplings for you before I go out."

"You don't have to—"

"No, I want to. And I don't have to be anywhere until ten."

"Where are you going tonight?" he asks.

"Meeting Holden and Carrie."

"Holden—I think Vince has mentioned him before?"

I nod briskly, somewhat uncomfortable with the mention of Cedric's brother.

Then I head to the kitchen and grab the dumplings out of the freezer. I already ate dinner, but I don't know when Cedric will offer me his grandmother's dumplings again, so I take advantage of this opportunity and add two for myself, in addition to the ones for him. I also make him a cup of tea, and I bring everything to him on a tray when it's ready.

He's typing furiously on his computer, and I stand in the doorway for a moment.

Seeing him deep in concentration is hot.

At the same time, I'm envious. I'm not dedicated to anything like that. He had a rough time writing for years, yet he kept at it.

Now the words seem to be flowing, and I'm just glad I get to see him like this.

After I deliver these dumplings, I'll get out of his hair.

Speaking of hair…

As I set the tray down on his desk, I have an urge to smooth the piece of his hair that's sticking straight up and disobeying gravity. Why does his hair always do that?

I find it oddly charming.

"Thank you." He winks at me.

Or maybe he just had something in his eye?

I'm generally good at telling the difference between someone flirtatiously winking at me and trying to get something out of their eye, but now I'm uncertain and flustered, which isn't like me at all.

"I might be home late," I say, "but, uh, tomorrow then?"

In my bedroom, I get dressed for my night out. I put on a Tom Ford suit with a blue shirt from Ascot Chang and a tie. After fixing my hair, I'm tempted to ask Cedric what he thinks but decide to leave him in peace.

The swanky lounge where I'm meeting my friends is on the forty-second floor of an office building. As I walk inside, I think back to the day I was here with Vince about a year ago. He left abruptly after getting a text. It must have been from Marissa, though he didn't tell me that at the time. I thought he seemed a little off that day, but he insisted he was fine.

Me, on the other hand? I went home with another man. Can't even remember his name.

I find Carrie Lo and Holden Khoo on some armchairs by the window. They're looking out at the city—it's a pretty nice view from here. I give them each a hug.

"You look great," I tell Carrie. "Love the dress." It's silver and perfectly fitted for her.

"What about me?" Holden asks jokingly. "You're not going to tell me that I look great?"

I cuff his shoulder and take a seat. "You don't need the ego boost. You're annoying enough as it is."

He doubles over in laughter.

A server approaches with a wineglass and pours me some pinot noir from the bottle my friends were drinking.

"Mmm," I say. "This is really good."

"It is, isn't it?" Carrie says.

"You know what else you'll think is really good?" Holden elbows me, then inclines his head to the left.

I know exactly who he means.

There's a willowy white woman with a pixie cut, and I feel a stirring of interest, but not enough to go over there.

"Maybe later."

Holden looks at me in shock.

"What?" I say. "I just got here. I want to hang out with you two for a while."

"Usually, you'd go up to her and invite her over here."

I shrug. "Later."

Unfortunately, Holden is still suspicious. "When was the last time you had sex?"

I think back. "A month ago?"

The day of the gala.

I haven't attempted to hit on anyone since then, which is unusual for me.

My lack of sex life probably has something to do with my new roommate. Though I told Cedric that I might have overnight visitors on occasion, it still feels awkward when he's living with me. Going to the other person's place or a hotel is always an option, however.

I open my mouth to tell Holden and Carrie about the roommate situation, but then I close it. For some reason, I don't want them to know. Am I afraid that they'll tease me about Cedric? That Carrie will ask if our Valentine's Day date went really well?

Yeah, that must be it.

Alright, I should think about ending my dry streak, but that woman with the pixie cut isn't quite doing it for me today. I continue to look around the room. No one catches my attention.

What do I want?

I imagine running my hands through dark, untameable hair and distracting Cedric from his writing…

No, not when he's finally gotten past the fifth chapter. I would keep him supplied with food and water (or coffee and tea) as long as he wanted to write, and then afterward, I'd take him to my bedroom…

No! What if it made things weird?

"You know who you remind me of?" Holden doesn't give me a chance to respond. "Vince. When he started seeing Marissa. Before he told us about her and how she was pregnant, remember how he was acting strangely? We had a bet that he was in love, which I won."

My lips twitch. "Yeah, you did."

Carrie looks at me sympathetically.

She knows about my crush on Vince. Holden doesn't, and I have no intention of telling him. But even when I had a crush on Vince, I had no trouble flirting with other people and sleeping with them.

Had a crush. Past tense.

Huh. It had definitely been fading, but now, I think it's actually gone.

Thank fucking God.

"So?" Holden says. "Am I right? Are you in love?"

"No," I scoff. "Definitely not."

"Good."

I have the weirdest sensation that I just told a lie, which I don't understand. I'm not in love. Besides, lying doesn't usually bother me because I spent so many years lying to my family on a regular basis.

Why does it bother me that I feel like I told a lie even though I *didn't* tell a lie?

I shake my head, attempting to clear it of that thought, and for the rest of the evening—until we head out at two—I manage to focus on my friends. For the most part.

But occasionally, I can't help wondering how Cedric is doing, if he's still writing or if he's gone to bed.

When I return home, I'm not surprised that all the lights are off, though I'm still disappointed. I flick on the kitchen lights and pour myself a glass of water, and that's when I see something unexpected on the kitchen island. A sleek navy box, embossed with a familiar logo and tied with a burgundy bow. There's a tag with my name on it, and on the back are two scrawled words: *Thank you.*

I open the lid to reveal three chocolates from Peony, a fancy chocolatier in the Distillery District. These colorful, semi-spherical chocolates are works of art. I recognize one as their Vietnamese coffee, and another is cassis. The last one, according to the label, is five spice.

In between all the writing Cedric's been doing, he got this for *me*. And if you think these chocolates are a generic gift, you've clearly never had the pleasure of eating something from Peony.

I can't help feeling a little giddy, and I'm pretty sure it has nothing to do with the wine.

They're nearly too pretty to eat, but I pick up the Vietnamese coffee chocolate and take a bite, and it's the best Peony chocolate has ever tasted to me.

And that, let me tell you, is impressive.

[13]

CEDRIC

MY GRANDMOTHER PUTS down her chopsticks and gives me a curious look. "You are looking happier today, Cedric."

"Am I?"

She nods decisively.

Well, if it's that obvious, I might as well tell them.

"I started writing again," I say. "In fact, I've written a hundred pages in the last two weeks."

I glance around the table. I'm at my parents' house for Sunday dinner, and my brothers and their families are here, too. Everyone seems happy for me, but I brace myself for the dreaded question.

"What's it about?" Dad asks.

And there it is.

It's amazing how you can spend two weeks working on something and be unable to give a one-sentence description.

But even if I'd thought up a catchy logline…

"I don't want to talk about it yet," I say, "but it's different from what I usually write."

"Will you have a pen name?" Po Po asks. "This is something I've heard about."

"I'm not at that point yet. But maybe."

"Did you use any of my cool ideas?"

I hesitate for a beat too long. "Well—"

"Ah, you did!" She claps her hands. "I knew it. The talking dumpling idea is amazing."

"Dumpy!" Evie exclaims from her high chair, holding up a noodle in one tiny fist.

"Are you really writing about talking dumplings?" Vince asks. "Do they, like, have a battle with some talking empanadas? Is it a children's book?"

"No," Po Po answers for me. "It is a sophisticated metaphor, right, Cedric?"

I shake my head. "There are no talking dumplings in my book."

"Did you take my other idea? About the grandma putting marijuana in her dumplings?"

"Are all your ideas about dumplings?" Vince asks.

Seeming to sense that I don't want to talk about this anymore, my mother turns to me and says, "How's the new apartment?"

"You moved?" Julian asks.

"I did."

"And he has a roommate!" Po Po says. "It's Brian Poon."

"Brian?" Vince sounds angry. "I told him not to pull anything with you."

"He's not *pulling* anything," I say. "We're friends."

Po Po clucks her tongue. "I still worry he will be a bad influence."

My head hurts. "Stop it. Please. He's not dragging me out to nightclubs at all hours, or whatever you imagine. He's not crossing any lines."

"I *told* him," Vince mutters again.

"We're getting along well, and *nothing* has happened."

This continues for…a while.

Perhaps I should have talked more about my book instead.

~

When I get home that evening, Brian is emptying the dishwasher.

"I need a drink," I say.

My roommate immediately goes over to the sideboard and pulls out a bottle of scotch and a bottle of bourbon. "Which are you in the mood for? Or wine? I have a nice merlot…"

"Bourbon." I'm just choosing at random. Any alcohol will do.

He pours the liquor, and I take a seat on the couch. He perches on the armchair.

"My family knows I started writing again after moving in with you," I say, "but they're still concerned about you being a bad influence on me." I pause and swirl the liquid in my glass. "I wonder if it's partly because I only came out last year. It feels like they're treating me as though I'm new to sex and romantic relationships."

"You'd probably been questioning it for a long time before you told them."

"Well, not *that* long." I pause again and have a sip of bourbon. "A few years back, I went traveling for several months. In Australia, I met a British guy—"

"And you fell in love with his accent?"

I chuckle. "He was alone, as was I. We decided to travel together. I was spending all my time with him, and I…fell in love, which was rather confusing for me. He was gay—he'd told me that near the beginning—but I'd only ever been interested in women."

"Whereas I was giving blowjobs at my all-boys high school. I knew early on. Not that there's a right or a wrong way to realize it."

"You see, I…"

I shut my mouth, debating whether to tell him something I haven't told anyone. While Brian and I have certain things in common, I highly doubt this would be one of them. He would *not* know what it's like.

But as I look at him over my glass of bourbon, I have the urge to tell him things.

"Later," I say, my voice scratchy, "when I was back in Canada, I read an article about demisexuality, and I identified with a lot of it. But several of the comments were like, 'Isn't that just normal? Why do we need a name for it?'"

"Never read the comment sections. You should know that by now."

I chuckle again. "And I remembered what it was like, especially back in high school and university. Friends talking about random people whom they thought were hot, and I...I felt like I had to *teach* myself how to participate in those conversations. Like, I had to teach myself to find women attractive when they were strangers to me. The idea of one-night stands, the idea of meeting someone at a bar and a few minutes of talking leading to a kiss and going home together...as a man, I felt like I should be excited by the idea, but it left me cold. It was more than simply not being interested in casual sex with women, though, but I didn't think I was gay. I still liked women, just not in the same way as my peers."

I sip my drink and try to find words for something I've never thought about clearly.

"Maybe being demisexual," I say, "is why it took so long for me to realize I don't only like women. I was never sexually interested in a guy until I fell in love with Nigel."

"Such a British name. What happened with him?"

"We were in New Zealand—Queenstown, to be exact—and he kissed me. And it was, well. It was everything. We delayed the next leg of our journey and spent a lot of time in bed." I can't help blushing. "I started to wonder about the future, about how it would work since we lived on different continents. Then he dropped a bombshell. He had a boyfriend."

Brian shuts his eyes and shakes his head before having a long swallow of his drink.

"He was quick to assure me," I continue, "that they were in an open relationship and he was doing nothing wrong. But we'd been traveling together for a month. Spending all day, every day together. The fact that he'd never told me this important piece of information before kissing me…it felt like a huge betrayal. Shouldn't it have come up in conversation at least once or twice? It felt like he'd purposely avoided mentioning his boyfriend. I couldn't help thinking he must be lying—the friends I know in open relationships wouldn't act like he did. And even if he was telling the truth, I'd always known I didn't want that kind of arrangement. Not my thing. I just wanted me and one other person, and Nigel said I should be more open-minded, and…"

"What did you do?" Brian asks.

"Flew to Thailand. Didn't tell him where I was going." I laugh.

I think it's the bourbon. It's making me light-headed, although I usually wouldn't feel alcohol this quickly.

"Anyway." I put down my glass and stretch out on the sofa. "That's how I realized I was bi and started wondering if I was on the ace spectrum. When I'm in a relationship, I enjoy having sex regularly, it's just…I'm not attracted…" I make some kind of hand gesture that's supposed to mean I-don't-know-what.

"I'm glad you understand yourself better now, even if you're not entirely sure which words to use."

I didn't want Brian to say much; I just wanted someone to listen. And he did that. Didn't bombard me with questions, which is what I'm certain my family would do, or make me feel weird for talking about it.

"Thank you," I say.

However, that simple phrase makes an awkwardness descend on the room, an awkwardness that wasn't there when I was talking about Nigel.

"And thank *you*," he says eventually. "For the chocolates. They were delicious."

I was a bit surprised when he didn't say anything yesterday, but also relieved. It had been an impulse buy; I'd been in the area, and I'd seen the chocolatier, and I'd thought of him.

"Oh. Yeah," I stammer.

"How did you know Vietnamese coffee and cassis are my favorites? Lucky guess?"

"Uh, no. I saw them on your Instagram a while back." Actually, it was an old post, from late last year. I'd scrolled back when I had nothing better to do.

The awkwardness…it's still there. Is it weird that I bought him chocolates? I thought he deserved something nice, with all that he's done for me. But maybe…

I stand up. "I should go to bed. See you in the morning."

When I crawl into bed, I don't immediately fall asleep. Instead, I keep thinking of Brian. I didn't hear any movement in the hallway, so I assume he's still sitting in the living room.

Did he pour himself more bourbon? What's he thinking about, and why do I want to know so badly?

I briefly wonder if the feelings I have for Brian are similar to how I once felt about Nigel, then quickly dismiss the idea.

That's not possible, right?

[14]

BRIAN

It's the Easter weekend, and Winnie is in town.

My sister is a lawyer in D.C., as is her husband, who has taken their kids to see her in-laws for the weekend while she visits me in Toronto. Winnie is the only person in my entire family—including many aunts, uncles, and cousins—who has a relationship with me. Nobody wants to anger my father by talking to me now.

But Winnie doesn't give a shit. Her husband's family is filthy rich, so she doesn't have to care about my father's money, but I like to think that even if she weren't well-off, she'd be on my side.

She's still in contact with our parents and older brother, though. It's mostly for my mom's sake, and so Winnie can work on convincing my father to make changes to his business practices.

Although I'm glad to see her, glad to be out having sushi with her on a Saturday night, it's still painful. I can't help thinking about all that I don't have.

Even before I was outed—by a cousin, in fact—everyone had given up on me meeting expectations. Like, when I was twelve. They thought growing up in Toronto and attending good schools should give me every advantage, and I constantly proved them wrong.

I have a gulp of my sake.

Earlier today, it was easier to forget. Winnie and I went on a long shopping trip together and spent ages in Holt Renfrew. She's an excellent shopping companion.

But now there are no pretty scarves to serve as a distraction.

"So, what's new with you?" She's asked me this question more than once today, but I kept deflecting.

"Not much." I shrug. "Going out, having fun. You know how it is."

"Nothing new? Nothing at all?"

"Well, I've been learning to bake."

"Ooh, when I come over for brunch tomorrow, will it feature some of your baking?"

"Yes. And by the way, I should warn you that I have a roommate. He'll likely be around. That's why you're staying in a hotel rather than my guest room, because I don't have a guest room anymore." I might be talking a little quickly. I don't know why.

"A roommate," Winnie says in a strange voice.

"Yes, a roommate. Not whatever you're imagining."

Winnie doesn't say anything else about my roommate whom she thinks is more than a roommate, and on Sunday, she comes over for brunch as planned.

Cedric eats with us, after I assure him that no, it wouldn't be any trouble. I'd feel weird if he carefully kept to his bedroom and office the whole time, especially since he's been subjected to all my trial runs at eggs hollandaise. Monday's version had various issues; Tuesday's wasn't bad. I gave him a break from it on Wednesday, and then Thursday, I finally got it right.

Today, it's just as good as Thursday's version, if I do say so myself. There are also blueberry orange muffins and a fruit salad.

"You made this?" Winnie asks in astonishment as I set a plate in front of her.

"You think I ordered the food, then made a mess in the kitchen just for fun?"

"I'd find that more believable, actually."

I make a face at her.

Cedric insists on sticking up for me. "He bakes multiple times a week. I often wake up to muffins coming out of the oven and…"

He trails off as I draw a finger across my throat.

He's trying to tell her that yes, I really do bake, but I know Winnie's thinking about the fact that I seem to be "playing house" with this man.

When he heads to the office to write, my sister gives me a sly look.

"After all these years of parties, are you settling down, Brian?"

"No, definitely not."

I say this a bit too forcefully, I guess, because she takes it as a sign of guilt.

I might enjoy her teasing if the man in question weren't Cedric Fong. The fact that Winnie is talking about me and Cedric in this way…it just seems wrong.

After brunch, she calls a car to bring her to the airport, then gives me an envelope, my Chinese name on the front. The writing is unmistakable, but Winnie tells me who it's from anyway. "Ma. She mailed it to me in secret."

"She could have mailed it directly to me," I say.

"I think she feared you'd throw it right in the trash if it showed up in your mailbox."

Fair enough.

"Just take it and read it," she says. "You don't have to reply."

"Don't worry, I won't."

Winnie gives me a hug. "Come visit in the summer. The kids miss you, and nobody will put a hamster in your bed this time, I promise."

And then she's gone.

That evening, Cedric is at his parents' house for dinner when I pour myself three fingers of whiskey and settle into the armchair with the letter.

I drink half the glass before I start reading.

My mother writes about how much she misses me, how she thinks about me every day, but my father has forbidden her from having a relationship with me.

Nothing I don't already know.

She makes it sound like I don't understand the situation. It's either him or me…and she can't leave him.

But they didn't even live in the same country for most of my childhood.

They were still married, though. They'd tell people that they were making sacrifices for the good of their son… Actually, I don't know exactly what they said, but it's easy to imagine.

Now…

God, is he threatening her? With what?

Money isn't an issue. If she leaves with nothing, Winnie or I could take care of her. But my father is a powerful man, and he can threaten with more than money—and get away with it. I don't know why that didn't occur to me before.

She goes on to say that if I marry a nice woman, all will be forgiven, etc. She's always struggled to understand why I couldn't pretend to be straight, since I do like women.

To be honest, I don't know what she truly thinks about my sexual orientation. When she talks about it, it's always all about how my dad feels. And I like to think she'd be somewhat accepting without that bastard, but maybe not.

Yeah, that seems more likely than the possibility of him threatening her, even if my father is a terrible person.

I look down at my glass. No more whiskey. I get up to pour

myself some more and bring the bottle to the coffee table with me. No sense getting up every time I want another drink.

I'm not sure how much I've drunk when Cedric comes in, a container of leftovers in his hands. His hair is being uncooperative again, and I itch to run my fingers through it.

"You okay?" He sits down on the couch, the corner closest to me.

I throw the letter on the table and gesture toward it. "It's from my mom."

"I can't read it. I only know a handful of characters."

Right. I forgot about that.

Well, probably for the best. I give him the short version. "Last year, word got back to my father that I slept with men, he disowned me, my brother stopped talking to me, my mother is forbidden from doing so, but she sent me a letter through my sister. Saying she misses me and such, but this is the way it is."

"I knew your family situation was…not good." He reaches out and squeezes my hand, which isn't something he usually does. He's usually only affectionate when he's drunk.

Then he stands up and gets himself a glass, and because I am who I am, I stare at his ass. When I'm rather tipsy—not drunk, but definitely buzzed—I tend to get horny.

Not that being horny is anything unusual for me.

He has a really great ass. I'd like to fuck him, but I know it's a terrible idea—and I also know he doesn't want to. Because love and fucking go together for him.

And he doesn't love me.

I feel a strange twinge in my chest, but that's not who we are to each other, no matter what Winnie thinks.

He pours himself a small amount of whiskey, then a larger amount for me, apparently sensing I need it.

"You're lucky," I say. "You just came back from a family dinner. Your parents still…"

"I know. I'm very lucky."

I usually downplay how much my family affects me. I'll laugh it off and get drunk.

Though I don't laugh it off tonight, I do take another swig of whiskey. It's not the best stuff I own—that would be wasted on me now.

"Carrie, too," I say. "Occasionally her family says thoughtless shit, but they mean well. And me…"

If I'd been the perfect son up until my father found out, would things be different? Would he have been willing to change his views for me?

Except I wouldn't *want* to be the sort of man he'd consider the perfect son.

But what am I anyway?

A waste of space, living off money I didn't make.

I'm not normally quite so down on myself.

Cedric seems unsure of what to say, and he squeezes my hand again. I wish I didn't enjoy that so much. I wish I didn't yearn for him to slide his hands to my belt buckle and get down on his knees for me.

"When my dad found out," I say, "he told my mother was that it was her fault, for naming me after a damn figure skater."

"Based on when you were born, it was either Brian Orser or Brian Boitano."

"Both." I shrug. "I don't know. That's how she learned the name, and she decided it would work as my English name."

Cedric leans forward. "I like you as you are. You know that, don't you?"

I'm not sure how to respond, except by pouring booze down my throat.

"Your dad is a piece of shit," he says.

"I know, but he's still my father."

Cedric squeezes my hand yet again.

We sit there in the dim light of the living room—*our* living room—drinking for a long time, but I slow my pace. I'd planned to get completely shit-faced to ease the pain of thinking about my family, to make it so I'd barely remember this tomorrow morning, but I've changed my mind now.

Just sitting here with Cedric, him squeezing my hand…

I don't want to forget this moment.

[15]

CEDRIC

April is a busy month for me.

I want to work on my book all the time, but it's the end of term. After this, though, I won't be teaching again until September, and my plan is to have my agent reading my book by August.

I spend a lot of time in the home office, marking and writing. When I'm not working, I see quite a bit of Brian. We hang out sometimes in the evenings, and he continues to make me breakfast every day. He gets us takeout every Friday, and it's always something good. Lobster, two ways—yes, he gets takeout lobster from a Chinese restaurant one night. Another time, it's a fancy charcuterie plate and lamb ragù with homemade pasta.

Though I keep trying to pay him back for the food, he won't let me, so instead I restock some of the liquor in his cabinet.

I feel bad that he's taking care of me. Not that I don't do my own laundry and clean up after myself, but he's always feeding me. I used to be pretty good at remembering to eat, but I'm so busy now that I sometimes forget…yet he always remembers, and he keeps the cupboard stocked with the instant noodles I like from H-Mart. He occasionally brings me treats throughout the day, too. Never in the mornings, once we've finished breakfast—he's continued to leave the apartment from eight thirty to eleven thirty every day, despite me telling him it's not necessary—but sometimes later.

One Tuesday, I set my alarm for more than an hour earlier than usual, and when I get out of bed, I feel almost like a kid on Christmas morning, even though I'm the one who's going to be doing the giving today.

I quietly move about the kitchen, getting out the ingredients for carrot pineapple muffins. When everything is combined—I'm pleased with myself for remembering not to overmix—I pour the batter into the muffin tin and pop it in the preheated oven.

Then I start on the coffee.

Brian emerges from the bedroom, and he looks around the kitchen in puzzlement.

"What is…"

"Surprise!" I say. "I figured I'd make breakfast for you."

He continues to look puzzled for a moment—perhaps because he just woke up—but then he smiles at me. "What are you making?"

"You'll see."

I tie an apron around my waist, something I probably should have done earlier, and pour us each some coffee. When the oven timer beeps, I remove the muffins from the oven. I let them cool for a couple of minutes before I start taking them out of the tin.

Well, attempt to take them out.

"Shit," I mutter.

"Is everything okay?" Brian asks from the other side of the kitchen.

I can't believe it.

I forgot to use muffin liners, which might have been fine…if I'd greased the pan. But I didn't do that, either.

I wanted to do something nice for Brian. I always appreciate it when I walk into the kitchen and find him making breakfast for me; I wanted to give him that same feeling.

So I'm practically crestfallen at one batch of ruined muffins.

"What's wrong?" Brian comes over and rests a hand on my shoulder.

"I forgot to line the tin," I mumble. "They won't come out."

"We can just take our forks and dig in. I'm sure the muffins will still be good."

But that wasn't the way I'd wanted it to go. I wallow in disappointment for a moment, and then I think of another idea.

"The tops are the best part anyway," I say, grabbing a knife.

Carefully, I slice off the tops of three muffins and place them on a plate, which I hand to Brian. It's not quite the breakfast I'd planned, but it'll have to do.

Coffee and muffin tops, plus the pomelo I peeled earlier.

Brian is smiling, and that makes it all worth it.

On Saturday afternoon, there's a knock on the office door.

"Come in," I say.

Brian walks in with another cup of coffee for me, plus a couple of biscotti. "I made them just for you."

Sometimes I think his voice is a bit flirty, but I'm sure I'm just imagining it.

"Cranberry and pistachio with white chocolate," he says. "You have to bake biscotti twice, did you know that? You bake them in flattish logs, then slice them up and bake them again."

"You can make me cookies that only have to be baked once. I don't mind."

He waves this away.

"Just learn from my mistake," I say, "and remember to grease the pan."

He chuckles. "What are you working on?"

"I'm researching types of poison. I hope nobody is, uh, watching my search history."

"This is for your cozy mystery?"

I nod. I haven't told him much about the book. Just that much. Although maybe…

My phone rings. I hold up a finger in Brian's direction and answer it.

"Hi, Po Po," I say.

"Ah, Cedric! You actually answered."

"Are you still holding that time I was in the shower against me?"

"You should know better than to shower during the hours I might call you."

"Po Po, I can't avoid it. You call me at all hours."

"You are lying," she says.

"No, on Monday you called me at ten in the morning, and last week—"

"Aiyah! You are nitpicking. Have you finished all the dumplings I made for you?"

"Yes, I had the last of them yesterday. They were delicious, thank you."

"I know they are delicious," she says. "I made them. But you aren't getting any more. Those were just for the bachelor auction. Am going back to dumpling retirement. Will sit on couch, eating candy and watching dramas all day! They give me many ideas for your books, you know. Maybe babies who are switched at birth?"

"No, I don't think—"

"This is the problem. You have still not told me what your book is about. Once I know, I can think of better ideas."

I know she'll keep badgering me if I don't provide any details.

I scrub a hand over my face and Brian laughs softly, which makes me smile despite the painful conversation I'm having.

"I'll tell you this much," I say to Po Po. "Right now, I'm looking up types of poison for use in my book."

"Wait, is there *murdering* in your book?"

"Yes, there is murdering in my book." I repeat the words in part so Brian will laugh again, and he does. It feels like we're a team, somehow.

"You are killing the poor innocent grandmother who makes good dumplings?"

"No, it's not the grandma who dies."

"But there is a grandmother?" Po Po asks. "Is she just like me?"

"I—"

"At least I know there is poison in your book. I will research poison for you."

"No, that's really not necessary…"

Brian holds out his hand, as though he wants my phone. Huh?

I move the phone away from my face and say to him, "You want to talk to my grandmother?"

"I can hear you!" she says.

Oh, dear.

I must have accidentally put it on speakerphone.

Brian nods, so I hand him the phone to deal with this mess. Not that it's his job to deal with my family, but if he wants to, I'm not going to stop him.

He takes it off speakerphone.

"No," he says into the phone, "I haven't read it either… I promise, I'm not lying to you… No, I'm doing my best not to be a bad influence… Really…"

He heads to the living room, leaving me with coffee and biscotti and the twenty-two tabs I have open, most of them about murder.

I've finished my research and returned to my manuscript when Brian enters my office again. He must have talked to my grandmother for at least fifteen minutes.

"What did you tell her?" I ask as he sets my phone on the desk.

"Oh, nothing. Just that you've been taking this researching

business very seriously and are trying out different types of poison on me—"

"You can't casually say stuff like that to my grandma! She'll bring it up in every conversation for the next six months!"

The office isn't huge, and he's standing close enough that I can reach out and give him the smack he deserves on his arm.

Unfortunately, I misjudge the distance and fall out of my chair.

The next thing I know, Brian is crouched on the floor next to me.

"You okay?" he asks.

"Yeah, I'm totally fine."

But even though I didn't hurt myself in that stunning display of clumsiness, I stay on the floor. I rather enjoy being here, next to Brian. Just the two of us.

For a moment, it's hard to draw air into my lungs, which I blame on the fall, even though I'm not injured.

"You sure?" he says.

"Yeah. Just bracing myself for the shit my grandma will give me at dinner tomorrow."

He smiles at me, and there's a dimple I've never noticed before.

Huh.

What else haven't I noticed?

I finally sit up and get back on my chair. "Well, uh…better go back to this writing business. The book isn't going to write itself, hahaha!"

He raises an eyebrow. "What have you been eating, drinking, or smoking for research?"

"Nothing," I manage to say with a straight face. "Nothing at all." I pause. "Agreeing to be your roommate was a good decision. I like living here with you."

"I like it, too," he says, closing the door.

My face feels warm as I return to my book.

$$[\ 16\ ]$$

BRIAN

"Where's Cedric?" Kris asks.

"He's busy," I say. "Unlike me, he actually has work to do."

"But it's Saturday night."

"I tried that argument, but he said the words were flowing."

It's interesting that my friends expect Cedric to join me every time now, as though we're a pair who always come together.

I look across the table at Ted and Michael.

"Here, try this." Michael pushes his beer toward his husband.

Ted smells it suspiciously before taking a sip. He makes an expression of disgust that sends Michael into a fit of laughter.

But then Ted smiles—well, what counts as smiling for him— and whispers something in Michael's ear.

I feel a pang of…envy?

That can't be right.

I've never thought a great deal about getting married. I mean, my parents' marriage didn't inspire me to have any positive feelings toward the institution, and I've always enjoyed being free to do whatever I like.

A wedding—to my exact specifications—could be fun though…

"Michael has the worst taste in beer," Ted mutters, but with fondness.

"This guy." Michael shakes his head. "He thinks he's sooo funny. Hey, want to see what my mother got Ginny?"

He pulls out his phone and shows us a picture of Ginny wearing a headband with goat ears and horns.

"She wears it *all* the time," Michael says. "Since Eli always wants to copy his big sister, he asked for a goat headband, too, but Ginny stomped her foot and said no, he was a copycat."

"How did you resolve it?" I ask.

"I told Eli that there are also unicorn headbands, and he decided he'd rather have one of those. Ginny said this was acceptable, as unicorns only have one horn, not two, so after school yesterday, we went to the dollar store to pick one out, and he's probably wearing it as we speak."

"Isn't it, uh, past his bedtime?" Kris asks.

"I suspect he's sleeping in it. It's rainbow-colored, which he thinks is very cool. The more colors, the better."

"I would never wear such a thing," I say. "It would mess up my perfect hair."

My friends laugh.

But I was lying. I'd wear one...for maybe thirty seconds, because it would amuse Cedric.

Ted and Michael head out at eleven thirty to relieve the babysitter. Normally, I'd consider hanging out with Kris for a little longer, but I don't want Cedric to stay up too late waiting for me. He never does that on weeknights, but he does on weekends, even though I tell him it's not necessary.

When I get home, he's where I expected him: sitting in the armchair, reading and drinking a cup of that blasted rooibos.

But even though I don't like his caffeine-free tea, I bought him a canister of vanilla rooibos, and I was far too pleased when he immediately made himself a cup and said it was delicious.

He closes his book and smiles at me as I slip off my shoes. "How was the beer? Tasty?"

I sit down on the couch. "Tolerable."

"How were your friends?"

"They're well."

"Want me to make some rooibos for you?"

I glare at him, which makes him laugh, and that brings me more pleasure than when Kris, Michael, or Ted laughs.

Cedric has been in a good mood lately. Occasionally, he's cross when he can't figure out something for his book, but mostly, he's upbeat.

Having a purpose in life probably helps.

I push away my dark thoughts and focus on how nice it is to come home to someone, rather than an empty apartment. And how nice his arms look in that T-shirt, and how his mouth is probably warm, especially since he just drank all that tea.

I always thought Cedric was cute, but I didn't anticipate how annoying it would be to keep fighting my attraction to him.

Like when he was standing at the counter waiting for water to boil earlier today, I admired how his shirt stretched across his back. I wanted to come up behind him, wrap my arms around his waist, and stand on my toes so I could kiss the crook of his neck. Then slide my hand inside his pajama pants and take his cock in my hand, feeling him harden for me.

I already know the answer to the boxers or briefs question. Not because he walks around in his underwear, but because I've seen his laundry sitting in the basket. However, I'd prefer to be pushing it down his thighs…

No. I need to stop having these thoughts. I usually don't spend so long obsessing about someone I can't have, with the exception of Vince. Either we fuck and I move on, or they're not interested and I move on.

But Cedric lives with me. Though I like living with him, maybe it wasn't the greatest idea.

"Something wrong?" he asks.

Damn him for being so observant.

I shake my head. "I'm tired. I'm going to call it a night."

"You okay? It's not even one. Early for you."

"I'm fine."

As I get ready for bed, I think back to my conversation with Holden and Carrie last month and realize what the problem is: I need to get laid. Usually this is one of my priorities in life, but it's fallen by the wayside lately.

Well, no longer.

Next week, I'm going to have sex. That's my resolution.

Hopefully, it will make me stop yearning to touch Cedric when he does innocuous things like boil water for tea.

[17]

CEDRIC

The End.

It's a Friday in mid-May when I type those beautiful words. Words I feared I'd never type again.

Sure, there are lots of problems with the manuscript. Ones I already know of and ones I'll find when I read it over in a few weeks. But for now, I'm finished.

I smile at the screen, back up the file in four different ways, and text Spencer. Then I head to the kitchen, where Brian is emptying the dishwasher.

"I finished my book," I say casually, as though it's not an enormous fucking deal.

Brian can see right through it. A spoon falls from his hands and clatters to the floor, and he gives me a hug.

"That's awesome," he says. "Congrats."

"I mean, it's only the first draft and—"

"No, it's awesome. We're going out tonight to celebrate, okay? No takeout."

I was kind of hoping he'd say that.

He proposes we go to an Italian restaurant on Queen, and I agree. If Brian suggests it, it's almost certainly amazing.

Sure enough, it is. I order linguine del mare; he orders ossobuco. To start, we share beef carpaccio, and the sommelier—a friend of Brian's, which doesn't surprise me—recommends a bottle of wine to us. For dessert, we split a lemon-basil panna cotta.

Everything is particularly bright and vivid and delicious today. I guess this is what happens when you finish a book for the first time in years.

I have an espresso with my dessert just because I feel like it, even though I wouldn't normally have caffeine this late. But I don't care if I can't sleep. At this point, I just want to stay up and smile.

Next, we head to the cocktail bar where Brian took me three months ago.

Weird to think of all that has changed since then.

As before, the idea of telling Naoki one or two things that I like and asking him to make his own creation is a bit overwhelming. I suddenly forget every type of alcohol that ever existed. But Brian murmurs something to Naoki, and I shrug and say I'll have the same.

I enjoy watching Naoki work. It's almost like a dance. Brian, however, is frowning—I have no idea why.

When Naoki puts our drinks on the bar, I hold up my glass and clink it against Brian's.

"Thank you," I say feelingly. "I'm not sure I could have written that book without you."

He smiles at me now. "You're welcome."

We lock eyes, and it's…disconcerting, to be honest. My skin prickles, and I don't know how to describe what I'm feeling.

Everything seems a little odd today.

I sip my drink. "Mmm. This is really good. It's sort of like an Old Fashioned, but there are cloves, I think? Maybe some other spice?"

Naoki looks up and nods at me.

Brian frowns again, then seems to purposefully wipe that frown away.

"Something wrong?" I ask.

"No. I'm happy for you. You gonna tell me what your book is about now?"

I try to shoot daggers with my eyes, but I'm sure I'm failing at looking angry today.

"It's supposed to be the first book in a cozy mystery series about a Chinese grandmother who lives near Chinatown in Toronto and frequents a karaoke dive bar. She's trying to make money to put her granddaughter through med school, and at the suggestion of a friend, she starts selling her dumplings infused with cannabis, except she comes across a dead body on her very first delivery…"

Brian tilts his head to the side, like he's trying to figure out whether I'm serious.

"And then the dumplings start talking," I say. "They give her clues in the form of elaborate limericks."

"Okay, you're shitting me."

"Until the talking dumpling part, I was entirely serious."

Now I feel nervous. He's going to think it's a terrible, wacky idea and…

I keep talking because I'm afraid of what Brian will say if given a chance to talk. "Cozy mysteries are often set in small towns, but I think Chinatown—"

The bastard interrupts me.

"It sounds like a lot of fun," he says. "I would like to read it, if you'll ever let me."

"Maybe, one day," I say nonchalantly, but I can't hide my smile. "Writing hasn't been fun for me, not like this, in a long time."

Brian doesn't say anything, but his expression is rather wistful.

"What's wrong?" I ask.

"Nothing."

"It's not nothing."

"Really, it is."

"Brian…"

"No," he says. "Tonight is about you. Not me."

I can't stand this.

The next time he puts his glass down, I grab it and hold it out of his reach. "I'm not giving this back until you tell me what's wrong."

This sort of behavior isn't like me, but I can't help it tonight.

He rolls his eyes. "I'll get Naoki to make me another one."

"He's pretty busy right now." The bar is more crowded than when we got here.

"Fine. I'll tell you. But you can't make a big deal out of it, okay?"

I nod, even though I'm not entirely sure I'll be able to keep that promise, and hand Brian his drink.

He has a sip. "I wish I was like you. You have something to do with your life. Something that gets you excited, something you want to do."

"You get excited, too."

"Not about anything meaningful, and I have no useful skills or talents. Now, please, let's talk about something else. What are you going to do now that you're done?"

I shake my head. "No, we're still talking about this. Don't you dare say you have nothing useful to offer."

"I eat and I drink."

"You're a very nice and thoughtful roommate."

He says nothing in response. I'm not sure if he believes me.

"Oh, come on," I say. "You make really good muffins and biscotti."

He waves this away. "Those are just little things, and it's not like I want to bake as a career. I did consider it. When you write in the mornings, you know what I do? I go for long walks, and I sit in coffee shops, and I try to figure out what the fuck I should do with my life. Doing the opposite of what my family wanted— that used to be enough of a purpose for me, but now…" He sighs. "Nobody should feel sorry for me, poor little rich boy that I am."

"You have lots of friends. You know people everywhere we go, and you always know *where* to go. I enjoy that about hanging out with you. I never have to make decisions."

"Those are hardly special skills."

"But I don't have them."

I wonder how many friends Brian really talks to, the way he talks to me.

I suspect it's not many.

"Listen," I say. "You're good at tons of things I can't hope to be good at. I honestly think you could…write a very good blog or something."

He gives me a look. "Your brilliant plan is for me to start a *blog?*"

"I know, I know, that wasn't a great idea. Restaurant reviews, maybe?"

He shakes his head.

Unfortunately, even though I'm on top of the world today and feel like I could do almost anything, I can't figure out how to solve his problem.

We only have one drink at the bar before heading home around midnight. Perhaps thanks to that espresso, I'm not in the mood for going to bed yet, so I make myself some vanilla rooibos and turn things over in my head.

People like Brian, and they like his parties, back when he used to throw them regularly…

"I've got it," I say. "I know what you should do."

I'm nearly as excited as when I typed *The End* earlier today. I know this is a really good idea, as good as my Chinese grandma amateur sleuth.

Brian looks at me skeptically as he walks over to the couch, but there's also something in his expression that seems... hopeful?

It almost knocks the wind out of me.

I didn't mean to take such a long, dramatic pause, but it's several more seconds before I can speak.

"You should be an event planner," I say.

"Like, weddings?" He sits beside me.

"If you want? I don't know. Charity galas. Parties for rich people. You used to do it for free, and I didn't go to your parties, but I've heard stories. And it's easy for me to imagine. You're well-connected. You have a good eye, and you know all about food. There are always issues that crop up at the last minute, and you'd be able to handle them calmly. You'd be excellent at that kind of problem solving, and like I said, you have an idea for everything. Even for Ginny's birthday, right? I'm sure you don't know much about farms, but that place stuck in the back of your mind. Consider it." I grab his hands to emphasize my point. "You'd be brilliant at it."

When I finally stop talking, my heart is beating quickly.

"What do you think?" I whisper.

"I think it could work, but I don't know how I'd get started."

"I don't, either, but I'm sure you can figure that out. And Courtney's sister, Naomi? She's an event planner. She does mostly corporate stuff, I believe, but I could arrange for you to talk to her. She might have more ideas."

"That would be great. Thank you." His voice is a little rough. I've never heard him sound like this before, and something inside me vibrates in response. "Nobody ever takes me seriously the way you do."

I want to say something lighthearted, but I can't get words out of my mouth. It feels like I used all my brainpower to tell him why he'd be a great event planner, and now there's nothing left.

The silence in the room is heavy, and somehow, it's drawing me toward him.

I put down my mug, but I never take my eyes off him. He's wearing a suit that looks very sharp. Probably some expensive brand that I should know but don't. His shirt is light purple, and purple is my favorite color on him.

When did I start having favorite colors for Brian?

Me, on the other hand—I never wear a suit jacket unless I absolutely have to, but I dressed up today in pinstripe pants and a blue dress shirt. I wanted to look nice for him.

I shift awkwardly on the couch. My skin feels hot, and I want…

As if in slow motion, I watch his hand come up, and he cups my cheek. When he strokes his thumb over my jaw, I moan. It feels so good when he touches me like that.

Then he leans forward.

He's going to kiss me. I've never thought of kissing Brian before, but suddenly, it's the only thing I want. The only thing that matters.

When he pulls back and drops his hand from my face, it's the worst.

No.

No, no, no.

He wants to kiss me, but he thinks I don't want it?

"Sorry, I—"

I cut him off by pulling him toward me and setting my mouth to his. For a moment, he doesn't move, but then his hands return to my cheeks.

He's kissing me back.

The gentle pressure of his lips against mine is perfect. When he increases the pressure, increases the pace, that's perfect, too. His hands are still cupping my cheeks, which makes me feel precious, somehow.

But I want more.

I remove his jacket and drape it over the back of the couch. Then I pull him onto my lap so he's straddling me, and I run my hands up and down his chest as we kiss each other.

It feels like everything has been leading toward this for a very long time, like some hidden part of me has been waiting for it— and I was too distracted by my book to notice.

I slip my tongue into his mouth, and the way he clutches my shirt and meets my tongue with his…it makes me feel a little more daring. I cup his ass in my hands, and then I pull back from him just a little so I can look at his face.

He really is a handsome man. How does he always look so polished, even when he's wearing an apron at eight in the morning and taking muffins out of the oven?

Yes, this man bakes for me! And he makes sure I do what's important to me, and he celebrates with me.

I press my mouth against his again, trying to get deeper, deeper. I tip my forehead against his and raise my hands to run them through his hair, to make it a little less perfect and more like mine, and I can't help wanting other things, too.

To feel the length of his naked body against mine. Skin against skin.

To be on my knees for him, to learn what it's like to have his cock in my mouth. How he looks when he comes.

I frantically unbutton his shirt as I continue to kiss him. I don't dare just pull—I'm sure it's an expensive shirt, and purple is my favorite color on him, after all.

At last, I spread the sides of his shirt apart and put my hands on his warm skin.

Oh, God, that feels good, and from his hiss, I gather it's good for him as well.

The next thing I know, he's lying on top of me.

中略

[18]

BRIAN

CEDRIC SAW ME.

That's how it felt. As if someone truly saw me for the first time—and liked what they saw. While he earnestly explained all the things he believes I'm good at...well, I just wanted to kiss him.

So, I touched him. Leaned in for the kiss.

Then I remembered he'd never shown the slightest interest in me, not in that way. Although I might stand behind him in the kitchen and fantasize about putting my hands on him, it was unlikely he did the same.

I pulled back. It was the right thing to do. The only thing to do.

Except then *he* kissed *me*.

And kept kissing me.

I've never been so glad to receive a kiss.

Now I have him reclined on the couch, and I'm on top of him, a position that's hardly a rare experience for me, though it's been a while.

I'd vowed to get laid so I could take my mind off Cedric, but it didn't work out. A couple of weeks ago, I started flirting with a man at a bar, but in the end, I couldn't do it.

Which isn't like me at all.

But now, I have Cedric underneath me, and it's everything I want. I start unbuttoning his shirt. He's a little bigger than me, which I love. Taller, wider, but not too sculpted.

I drop my mouth and trail a path up from his navel. I detour to swirl my tongue around his nipple, and oh, he likes that.

I won't forget.

This time when I kiss his lips, I can feel his skin underneath mine, and it's glorious. I rock my hips against his. I'm hard as stone, and he's hardening, too. As I grind myself against him, he shuts his eyes and groans.

Yes. Fuck, yes.

"Brian," he murmurs.

I kiss him more frantically as I rub myself all over him, unable to get enough. It probably has something to do with having a longer dry spell than usual…

I suddenly sit up and realize what I'm doing.

The one thing I swore I wouldn't do. Cedric is my roommate, and we've got a good thing going, and this could make it complicated. Plus, I promised Vince that nothing would happen.

After all, I usually just fuck people a few times and move on.

I hop off the couch, fold one side of my shirt over the other, and grab my jacket.

"Is something wrong?" Cedric asks, looking a little lost.

"I don't think this is a good idea." But those words barely come out, and they don't feel true. Because kissing him really did seem right.

Except I *promised*.

I rarely make promises; people don't usually expect much of me.

"We should at least…think about this," I tell him.

He nods, looking like he wants to say something more, but I

can't bear to stay here any longer. I hurry to my bedroom and shut the door behind me.

My skin is flushed, and my erection isn't going anywhere. I'm not sure I'll be able to sleep at all tonight, but I definitely won't be able to sleep unless I rub one out.

I quickly undress, then go to the en suite bathroom and brace one arm against the wall. I stroke myself with my other hand, imagining it's Cedric's hand on my cock instead. Then I imagine he's lying on his stomach, and I'm rubbing my cock against his ass and kissing the side of his neck, leaving marks that won't fade for several days. I imagine rolling him onto his back and sucking him off, making him feel better than he's ever felt before—my blowjob skills are pretty incredible, if I do say so myself.

I finish in my hand and clean myself off, feeling so damn pathetic.

I can't do anything right.

There was *one* person I wasn't supposed to fuck, and it almost happened anyway.

Why did I have to do that?

My attraction to him was nothing new, but I'd kept my hands to myself. Until it felt like he got me in a way nobody else did.

And as I put on some pajamas, I remind myself that he kissed me first.

Based on our conversation several weeks ago, Cedric doesn't go around kissing lots of people—unlike me—and if he kissed me…

I sit down on my bed and press a hand to my chest.

If he kissed me and started getting me naked, he must feel something for me, right? That's how it works for him, isn't it?

I *mean* something to him.

I let out a shaky breath.

Does he want a relationship? It's been a while since a person wanted that with me, but it's happened. Usually after they've slept with me a few times and start getting attached, maybe blown away by my incredible oral sex skills.

On the other hand, the only person I ever wanted like that was Vince.

Cedric's brother.

It's just like me to get myself into such a mess.

I'm about to turn out my light when I remember what I'm supposed to do tomorrow, and I swear under my breath.

I haven't been to Vince's new house before. Although he's lived here since before Lucas was born, we haven't seen a ton of each other in that time. But Holden's in town, and when he texted me last week and suggested we visit Vince, I didn't make excuses.

Vince is my friend. I shouldn't avoid this forever, right? Even if seeing him is a little weird and his life is completely different from what it used to be.

Unfortunately, as I take off my shoes and walk into his house, all I can think is, *I kissed your brother. I kissed your brother.*

I try not to look guilty.

The three of us sit in the living room and have some tea, which feels strange—when I'm with Vince and Holden, I'm usually drinking booze.

It's real tea, not that rooibos shit.

My lips twitch.

Vince looks at me curiously, but then his attention is drawn away by the babbling baby in his lap. Lucas must be…six or seven months old now? I can't remember.

"Do you want to sit with Uncle Brian?" Vince asks him.

Lucas makes some noises, which Vince apparently takes as a yes.

I put down my tea, and a moment later, I have a baby in my

lap. Lucas looks up at me as though he's trying to figure me out, which is rather alarming. Then he tugs at my ear.

"He's fascinated by ears these days," Vince says.

Well, then. I tug on Lucas's earlobe. Gently, of course.

Lucas starts crying.

"Sorry," Vince says. "I should have mentioned that he's only interested in other people's ears. He doesn't like it when his own are touched. As of last Friday."

I hand Lucas back to Vince because crying babies aren't my forte.

"It's okay," Vince says to his son. "Daddy's here. Uncle Brian didn't know any better, but he won't forget now. Why don't we show everyone your new trick?" He blows a raspberry.

Lucas giggles, then blows one back.

"See?" Vince says. "Isn't that cool?"

Lucas is cute, but this has confirmed the fact that I don't want a baby, who'd spit and throw up on my clothes.

And this visit has confirmed something else: Vince has no hold on my heart anymore. His happiness, in a life I never want for myself, isn't causing any painful stirrings in my chest. I'm simply glad for him; I harbor no jealousy toward Marissa. Maybe that's why I agreed to visit him today, after so many months of mostly avoiding his company.

When we leave Vince's and head back downtown, Holden asks if I want to go to a party that night, and I say yes.

However, I end up leaving the party at eleven.

I head to a hotel bar near home, one that's rarely busy. The bartender pours my usual bourbon—yes, I come here often—and I stare at the collection of bottles behind the bar.

Cedric gets me in a way that Vince never did. I can't deny how much I appreciate it. And I'm pretty sure he has feelings for me, feelings that aren't purely sexual. I don't see it as a complication I don't need; no, it makes me warm and fuzzy inside.

I have another swallow of bourbon.

Dear God. I feel special. Honored.

I want to continue making him breakfast every morning, and a whole lot more, and unlike with Vince, this isn't some hopeless, unrequited crush.

In a way, having a crush on Vince was safe because nothing could come of it. He wasn't interested in relationships, not until he met Marissa, *and* he's straight.

With Cedric, it's not that simple, and it has the potential to blow up badly, especially since I don't know what the fuck I'm doing.

But it doesn't feel hopeless.

This man who rarely kisses anyone—has he been with anyone since Nigel, that fuck-up?— kissed *me*.

I put my hands to my lips and smile.

I never would have imagined.

He got closer to me than people usually get, and rather than thinking there was nothing underneath my shiny surface, he concluded quite the opposite.

But I can't think about the event planner business now. That can wait. This seems much more pressing, especially given he's my roommate, and when I made him breakfast this morning, we couldn't meet each other's eyes.

If I want a relationship with Cedric, that's not breaking my promise to Vince, right? Trying to make things work with Cedric isn't 'screwing around.'

But is a relationship what I want?

Surprisingly, it seems to be.

And come to think of it, I don't believe I ever really wanted that with Vince. It was just a safe fantasy. Because I knew it was impossible, I could desire him without truly wanting all that being together would entail.

With Cedric, it's different.

Before, I was thinking of fucking him, nothing more, but now everything is all tangled up. I want to kiss him good morning and good night every day. And we've lived together for more than two months without wanting to kill each other, which has to be a good sign for our compatibility. A low bar, perhaps, but still. It's something, for a person like me.

The more I think about it, the surer I am of my feelings, as unexpected as they are. I want him in a different way from how I usually want people.

Though I think the bigger issue is whether I can actually do this. I don't know shit about these sorts of things, let's be honest. The only time someone referred to me as their boyfriend, it was news to me. I freaked the hell out and immediately "broke up" with her.

I've never had a relationship.

I've never even had a proper fucking job.

But *he* sees more than that, and it makes me think maybe I can?

Corny, but it's true.

When a burst of laughter escapes my lips, several people in the quiet bar look at me.

I'm going to give myself a little more time to think this through, until I'm a hundred percent sure of what I want. I'll probably avoid home in the meantime because…

Well, this is awkward, and the many, many social situations I've been in haven't prepared me for it.

Seriously, orgies are much simpler than telling one person how you feel.

[19]

CEDRIC

It's a good thing I'm finished my book because I don't know if I could write now. Though at the same time, it might be nice to have something else to think about, something other than *him*.

It's been five days since we kissed—yes, I've been counting—and I've barely seen Brian in that time. Is he avoiding me?

I don't think this is a good idea, he said.

Because we're roommates?

Every evening at eleven, I drink rooibos in the living room, hoping he'll appear to insult my tea, but he's always out, doing who knows what. The awful thought occurs to me that maybe he's having sex with other people, and of course he's free to do that, but I don't like it.

I didn't realize how I felt until Saturday night. It snuck up on me out of nowhere.

But now, I think of the signs. The loopy grin on my face when I passed by Peony and decided to get a present for him. The way I look forward to seeing him every morning. The excitement I feel when checking his Instagram multiple times a day.

Maybe he's trying to figure out how to let me down.

I know sex and relationships go together for you, Cedric, but they don't for me and I'm not interested. Would you like some blueberry orange muffins with that?

It's ridiculous to care for him so much, especially given everything between him and Vince.

But Saturday night, he didn't act like someone who was simply horny and wanted to fuck. He never made a move until I told him he should be an event planner.

He continues to make me breakfast until Friday morning, when there's no smell of baked goods, no coffee, no movement in the kitchen. He's left me a note, though, telling me there are fresh coffee grounds in the French press and leftover muffins.

I eat my breakfast and drink my first cup of coffee while looking at my phone, and then I head to the office with the second cup. I look over at the other desk in the room. I never see him use it.

That's it. I can't stand this anymore.

I turn on my computer and start looking for apartments.

Yes, it's pathetic. My roommate didn't make me coffee and fresh muffins one day and I'm thinking of moving out. But I don't care that I had to boil water myself—I'm more than capable of that. It's just that things are awkward as hell, and I don't see how I'll move forward while I'm living here.

After a solid hour of searching, I've determined that the apartment situation is just as bad as it was a few months ago. Since I can't bear the thought of living with someone else right now, I'm looking for a one-bedroom, or a studio if necessary, and given my price range, I'll need to move far from downtown.

Damn, I really do have a good deal here.

I shouldn't have kissed him.

Still, I would have figured out my feelings at some point. But if I'd had the sense not to make a move, he wouldn't be avoiding me.

I shove my hands through my hair in frustration before

texting Spencer, just in case he has any ideas for where to live, though I don't tell him what happened with Brian.

Then, to avoid looking for apartments, I pull out my notebook and write down possible ideas for later books in my mystery series. At first, my mind keeps straying, but eventually, I beat it into submission.

I'm very much in my own world when a noise startles me. I knock over my mug, spilling a little cold coffee on the desk.

"Shit," Brian says from the doorway. He goes away, then returns with a couple of paper towels, which he uses to clean up the mess. "I didn't mean to scare you."

"No big deal. It barely touched the corner of my notebook."

He puts his hands in his pockets. "We need to talk."

Yes, we do. I'd hoped to have some new living arrangements before we did so, but this is for the best.

However, I delay it a little longer. I want to give myself a few minutes to prepare for him saying he doesn't care for me.

"I'm making tea first." I head to the kitchen. "You want some?"

"What kind? That awful shit that isn't actually tea?"

Well, this is refreshingly ordinary. For a moment, I wonder if we've returned to normal, and then I remind myself that he's about to break my heart.

Right.

A few minutes later, I sit down on the couch. He's not beside me on the couch today; no, he's in the armchair, tapping his fingers on the armrest.

This makes me more anxious. I can't wait any longer.

I blurt out, "Don't worry, I'm moving out."

He stills. "When? Where?"

"Haven't figured out the details yet, but I'll come up with something. My parents' house, if nothing else. I'm sure they'll be glad to bother me on a daily basis. It was very kind of you to let me live here for a few months, but it's uncomfortable now."

"I know, and I'm sorry about that."

"It's okay, I understand." I try to sound breezy, even if it's not natural for me. "We kissed, it was a big deal to me but not to you, and you're struggling to let me down gently. I'm sorry I ruined everything."

He looks at me in confusion. I'm used to him always knowing what to do, where to go, and now…

Eventually, he comes to sit on the couch next to me. "So, it *was* a big deal to you."

"I…yeah. But you like—or liked—my brother."

"I didn't realize you knew about that."

"I asked why he didn't see you much anymore, and he told me."

"You asked about me?"

"I was a little curious about you from the first time I saw you, but it's okay, I get it—"

"No." He speaks more forcefully than I've ever heard him speak before. "You definitely don't get it. I felt guilty because you're my roommate and I promised Vince that I wouldn't mess around with you. That's why I ended the kiss, even if it was one of the hardest things I've ever done."

I open my mouth, but no words come out. Did he really just…?

"But I want to try," he says. "With you."

"Try?"

"Try to have a relationship. Be your boyfriend." He places his hand on my cheek. "I don't know how to go about any of this, but I finally decided that I want it."

I swallow. "What have you been doing all week?" His Instagram has been strangely quiet—yes, I've been checking—so I have no idea.

"Sitting in bars and coffee shops. Thinking about you."

"While you avoided me."

"Like I said, I don't know what I'm doing." He pauses. "What do you think? You want to do this with me?"

I nod, and as soon as I do, he kisses me.

It doesn't start tentatively this time, and when he thrusts his hand in my hair, he murmurs, "I'm always thinking about touching your hair. It never behaves." His lips find mine again, like he can't stay away. "You want to know what else I think about doing? Well, perhaps I shouldn't tell you..." He presses himself against me, and he's hard.

I feel honored to be the object of his daydreams, but we still haven't finished talking about everything. "What about Vince?"

"I'm not in love with him anymore, and in some ways, he doesn't know me all that well. I promise, it's not an issue for me."

"Okay." I believe him.

"You're not going to move out?"

"No. Unless you think dating will work better if we don't live together."

"I like it like this, even if we did everything backward by moving in together before we started dating."

We're kissing on the couch like on Saturday, except this time, we know things we didn't know back then. I want to explore him and learn more, learn what gets him going. I kiss his earlobe, his forehead, the tip of his nose before moving back to his lips.

He pushes me back on the couch, and I go willingly, my head against the armrest. His legs on either side of mine, he grinds himself against me, and I moan.

"I want to take you out on a date tonight," he says—not the words I was expecting to come out of his mouth. "That okay? I already made reservations, hoping you'd say yes."

"Yes."

"But for now... Bedroom?"

I take his hand and lead us to his bedroom.

His is the bigger room. The one with a king bed, rather than a queen. The one with the en suite washroom. I've barely glanced in here since that first day, when he caught me looking inside.

We stand toe to toe; I'm a few inches taller than him. I watch as he removes my shirt, feeling separate from my body, like this can't really be happening. Like it's too good to be true.

Suddenly, I'm nervous. Brian is very experienced, and I'm…not.

I don't want to disappoint him.

"I haven't been with anyone in a long time," I say.

"Same here."

"Except a long time for you is like…three months."

"Something like that. I couldn't do it because I kept thinking of you. It pissed me off."

I can't help laughing.

But when he drops my shirt to the floor, my laughter fades.

His hands are all over my chest. He runs one up the middle, between my nipples, and the other goes around to my back.

"What's a long time to you?" he asks.

"A few years."

He doesn't snort like this is the most ridiculous thing he's ever heard. No, he's intent on touching me all over, and I feel horribly exposed, but at the same time, it feels really good. I arch into him, wanting to be as close to him as I can.

His hand skims downward and firmly squeezes my ass. "We can go as far—or not far—as you like. It's okay."

I start unbuttoning his shirt, which I toss on the floor on top of mine. Brian is lean and muscled, and it's no surprise he's comfortable like this.

He grins. "Like what you see?"

He's slightly cocky, but I can tell there's a thread of uncertainty running through him, even if he's gotten naked with many, many people before.

I feel like…we can take care of each other.

Still, I briefly remember the last time, with Nigel. The betrayal I felt afterward.

"You don't have a secret boyfriend or girlfriend, do you?" I try to make it a joke.

But Brian can see behind that, just like I could see behind his cocky grin.

"I promise," he says, all serious. "It's just you."

It's difficult to hide with him, but I think that's okay. Because I do trust Brian.

He topples us onto the bed, and God, it's nice to be underneath him. Our hands are all over each other as we kiss, but even as he grabs my ass, there's no move to get under the rest of my clothes.

I guess he's waiting for me to make the first move.

I can feel his cock, even if I can't see it. I think of having him in my hand. In my mouth.

Unable to wait any longer, I unbutton and unzip his pants, slip my hand into his underwear, and give him an exploratory stroke. When he shudders, it makes me smile.

I crave his reactions. He has an indescribable power over me.

I hiss out a breath as he undoes my pants and slides his hand inside, making contact with my erection.

"Good?" he asks.

"Yeah."

I haven't had anyone touch me in so long, and it feels so right that it's him.

For a minute, we just touch each other, and when I can't stand it any longer, I start kissing him, feeling this unbearable need for his mouth on mine. He runs one hand through my hair, and I'm mesmerized by everything he does, by every touch—how does he make it all feel so great?

I sit up and tear off the rest of his clothes, and he does the same to me, and then we're rolling around naked together.

When he suddenly withdraws, I think of last Saturday, on the couch, and I'm the tiniest bit afraid it's going to end now, but instead, he reaches into his night table and pulls out…a piece of paper?

"From a few weeks ago," he says. "Just so you know."

I skim it, forcing myself to comprehend words right now.

He doesn't have any STDs.

He takes the paper and returns it to the drawer, and then he's kissing me again, rubbing his cock against mine... Oh God, that feels amazing.

I press kisses down his body, down, down, down... I'm salivating at the thought of having him in my mouth. When I wrap my hand around his cock and swirl my tongue around the tip, he's already rubbing a hand over his face as though it's too much, he can barely stand it.

I don't have much experience with cocks other than my own, but I love his. It's long and curves slightly to the left.

I take him in my mouth, and his hips jerk.

Yes, doing this to him is as good as I imagined.

I cup his balls before returning my hand to his shaft, and then I move my mouth up and down on his cock, enjoying the way it fills me, the way I can't quite take it all.

My other hand moves to my own erection. I can't stop stroking myself while I have my mouth on him, and I can tell from the way his eyes darken that he likes this.

"Cedric." He shoves his hands through my hair and pulls me upward. "It's so hot when you touch yourself," he murmurs, and then he kisses me again as he jerks me off. "I won't last much longer."

I move my mouth back down to his cock, wanting to swallow. He explodes almost as soon as I wrap my lips around him, and it doesn't take many strokes before I come.

I lean back on my heels and regard him.

He's a mess, and I love it.

"Let's have a shower," he says.

I've never actually been in the en suite before. It's more luxurious than the other washroom, and the shower fixture seems fancy, but that's about all I register.

Because I'm having a shower. With Brian.

His hands are soaping me all over, and when he slides his hand over my crack, I'm suddenly very still.

"You like a finger up your ass when you get a blowjob?" he asks.

I nod quickly, and he chuckles. He keeps touching me, running his hands over my ass cheeks and squeezing as we kiss under the spray.

When we emerge from the shower, he towels me off, and it reminds me of how he bakes and makes coffee for me. Takes care of me.

"I really like you, you know," I say.

"I know. Now let me show you how much I appreciate that."

He presses me against the wall, then gets down on his knees. My cock is soft when he takes it in his mouth, but it's not long before I'm hard. He keeps his mouth on me as he reaches into a drawer and pulls out some lube. He squeezes some on his finger and slowly circles my hole before pushing inside.

"Do you touch yourself here?" he asks.

"Sometimes."

"With toys?"

"I have…a couple."

He smiles at me before he returns to sucking my cock. Then he touches my gland, and I nearly jump.

When he smirks, I half want to push him back on the floor, take his cock between my lips, and wipe that smirk off his face. But I'm enjoying myself a little too much to do that. It's obvious Brian is more skilled at this than I am.

"I'm going to…" I don't even finish that sentence before I'm coming in his mouth.

A few hours ago, I thought I'd have to move out, and now…

[20]

BRIAN

AT SEVEN THAT EVENING, I'm sitting on the couch, scrolling through my phone as I wait for Cedric.

He emerges at last, tugging at the lapel of his suit jacket.

I haven't seen him wear a suit since the bachelor auction. He looks slightly uncomfortable, but I'm touched he did this for me.

I saunter over to him, acting more confident than I feel.

He gestures at my purple tie. "I, um. I like that color. It's my favorite color on you."

I can't help laughing, but he scratches the back of his neck and looks even more uncomfortable.

"Sorry," I say. "I just…nobody's ever said anything like that to me before. But I'm glad you like me in purple. Very *royal*. You look good, too. You fill out that suit nicely."

"It feels tighter than I remember. Must be all those muffins you bake for me." He buttons the top button on his jacket. "Is yours…Armani?"

I look at him in horror. "This looks nothing like my Armani suit."

He shrugs. "It's the only brand I know. I assume all nice suits are Armani."

I can't believe I find his blasphemy adorable.

We head to a restaurant on Bay Street. It's one of two Moroccan restaurants in the vicinity, but this is by far the superior one. The other feels touristy and the food is an afterthought, which isn't a good thing to say about a restaurant, but it's true.

We share two tagines. The chicken tagine has green olives and preserved lemons; the lamb tagine has prunes and figs. When I lift the lids off the tagine pots, the incredible smell wafts toward me, and Cedric looks eager to try them.

This isn't the first meal we've shared at a restaurant together, just the two of us. For starters, there was dim sum and lobster on our so-called Valentine's date.

But we'd been clear that wasn't really a date. Unlike today.

And now I know what it's like to have his hands and mouth all over me.

For dessert, I take Cedric to my favorite Japanese cheesecake place downtown, Cheese & Me. As we're waiting in line, I see someone familiar. I think he used to do landscaping at my house back when I lived on the Bridle Path. Peter, that's his name. I'm about to say hi to him, but he seems too focused on the woman beside him to notice.

Cedric and I get a double fromage cheesecake because that one's the best—I prefer the plain double fromage cheesecake over the matcha and chocolate versions. We find a cramped table at the back. Our knees bump against each other, since there isn't much space, and I can't say I mind. I cut us each a quarter of the small cake, and before I take my first bite, I notice something distracting about Cedric.

"Your hair is defying gravity again," I say.

"You mean it's sticking straight up."

We're in the corner and nobody is paying attention to us, so I reach over and smooth it down. But as soon as I remove my hand, his hair is back to doing its own thing.

I wonder how much wilder it'll look later tonight.

Unable to help myself, I rub my lower leg against his, and his sharp intake of breath, though quiet, is gratifying. Causing someone to make such sounds is nothing new to me, but for some reason, it's way more gratifying when it's *him*.

And when I put my fork in my mouth and he stares at my lips, that's nice, too.

I wonder what he's thinking about. Is he remembering how my mouth felt on him?

God, it's nice not to feel guilty about having such thoughts.

When he starts eating his cheesecake, I'm equally entranced. I'm not sure I've ever been so turned on by someone eating *cheesecake* before, though I've been turned on by lots of things over the years.

I steal a bite of cheesecake off his plate.

"Hey!" he says. "Eat your own damn cheesecake. You've got a perfectly good piece sitting in front of you."

"But yours is better."

He scoffs.

"Because it's *yours*," I say.

We look at each other for a long moment before I speak again.

"After this, we're going home."

I'd planned on taking him to Lychee for drinks, a throwback to Valentine's Day, but I don't have the patience to sit across from him any longer.

I want to get him naked again.

Some people have rules about spending the night together.

My friend Holden is one of them. He never spends the night with a woman.

But me?

I haven't made any such rules.

So, I'm not unused to waking up with someone else in my

bed, though it's been a few months since this has happened and there are many differences from usual.

First of all, it's my roommate who's in my bed, rather than someone I met at a bar or a nightclub or a party.

Second of all, we went on an actual date last night, and there was no confusion on the matter. We both knew it was a date.

Third of all, he slung an arm around me when he briefly woke up half an hour ago, and I haven't moved it.

Shocking behavior on my part.

Usually, I get rid of the other person quickly the next morning. Well, maybe not too quickly if they want to have sex again, but I wouldn't dare let them cuddle me, and I wouldn't dare actually enjoy it.

But I remind myself that this is okay.

Except after years of avoiding any kind of serious attachment, my instincts tell me otherwise.

Sex used to be about having fun and getting off. Nothing more.

And now, for the first time, I'm trying *more*, and doubts plague me again.

Cedric is smiling slightly in his sleep. He might be three years older than me, but he looks so innocent when he's sleeping like this, his arm around me. I'm touched that he can sleep so peacefully in my bed.

Why am I watching him sleep, like a weirdo?

What will he think if he wakes up and catches me staring at him?

I don't think he'll regret yesterday. He seemed pretty sure about it, and I give pretty great blowjobs, if I do say so myself.

It's not so much the sex stuff I'm worried about.

It's everything else.

What if yesterday was our one perfect day together, and that's it?

I can't seem to relax in bed with him, so I get up and start what has become my routine in the past few months.

After getting dressed, I head to the kitchen, where I pull up the recipe for oatmeal raisin cookies on my phone. Cedric said these were his favorite cookies.

I've found being in the kitchen first thing in the morning—to do more than just stuff toast in my mouth—relaxing. I don't always bake something, but I always set up breakfast for him.

And now that everything has been turned upside down, it feels good to keep my routine.

The cookies come out of the oven, and Cedric still isn't awake. I wring my hands, not sure what to do with myself. I used to be better at doing nothing, but I can't seem to manage it now.

Blueberry orange muffins it is!

I make these almost once a week, so I don't need to look at the recipe, and there's a certain peace in measuring out the ingredients, mixing them together, lining the muffin tin, and pouring in the batter.

It's something I can do, and it's good to feel competent.

When I take the muffins out of the oven, Cedric still hasn't emerged. It's almost ten, and he never sleeps this long.

I tiptoe back to my bedroom. He's asleep, his arm thrown over the other side of the bed.

I pace around the living room for five minutes before returning to the kitchen. I start boiling water for coffee, even though he's not awake yet, and after staring at the kettle, I search for another recipe on my phone.

Ah, yes. The lemon poppyseed loaf I've been meaning to try.

One of the things I like about baking is that it provides immediate returns. In a short period of time—I don't make anything too complicated—you get a finished product that you can consume.

The lemon poppyseed loaf is in the oven and I'm sipping my coffee when Cedric finally appears, wearing boxers and a T-shirt.

The fact that he hasn't put on pants seems like an acknowledgement of last night.

I pour him some coffee. He's not fully functional until he's had some coffee, although perhaps today will be different since he slept for ten hours.

"Thanks," he says. "I was hoping you'd still be in bed when I woke up, but I slept for a long time." He looks around the kitchen and whistles. "Are you stress baking?"

"I wouldn't call it *stress* baking. I'm not stressed."

He raises his eyebrows. Then he wraps his arms around me from behind like it's the most natural thing in the world. "You're bad at morning-afters?"

"Not usually. I've had a ton of them, after all."

"What's wrong? Did I do something?"

That's what makes me confess the truth. I can't bear for him to believe he's at fault.

"Of course not," I say. "You were great. I just…I don't know how to be in a relationship. I've never really tried, and I don't have any good examples in my life. I don't even know what a healthy relationship looks like."

"What are you talking about? I mean, I know your parents—"

"And my brother and his wife."

"Okay," he says, "but what about your sister?"

"I'm not really sure what their marriage is like."

"Think outside of your family. Like, Michael and Ted."

Cedric has a point. They seem happy together, and they've been married for nearly ten years.

"Even if you don't know much about romance," he continues, "you know what good friendships look like."

"A lot of my friends don't know me very well." *Not like you do.*

Cedric shrugs. "You act like you have no idea about these things, but I don't think that's true. And if there are any problems, I'll be honest with you and we'll work it out, okay?"

He really does have faith in me. It's kind of incredible.

"I'm sorry I asked if you had a secret boyfriend or girlfriend," he says. "That wasn't about you. That was about me and my insecurities after Nigel. But I didn't truly think it was a possibility. There was just this nagging voice at the back of my mind."

"I knew it wasn't about me." I pause. "How many girlfriends have you had?"

"Three."

Not a ton, but it's still a hell of a lot more than my relationship history.

I want to kiss him, and I no longer have to hold myself back when I have such urges. I wrap my arms around his neck, back him up against the refrigerator, and kiss him hard, taking comfort in his touch as well as his words.

When we finally come up for air, he smiles at me and says, "What are we going to do with these baked goods? I can't eat *all* of them."

I think for a moment. "How about we bring them to Ted and Michael? I'll see if they're around. You want to come with me?"

He smiles at me again, and shit, that makes me smile in response.

He's pretty cute.

As Cedric drinks his coffee and eats his muffin, I check on the lemon poppyseed loaf and text Michael, who says they'd be happy to have us visit. Then I help myself to a muffin. Cedric and I have eaten breakfast together many times, but now, everything is different.

I definitely feel better than I did when I was furiously mixing batter earlier, but I'm still a little unsure about the whole thing. He believes in me, but what if that belief is misplaced?

With every passing moment, though, I want to make it work even more badly, even if I think he deserves someone who's less of a mess.

And then there's the fact that our lives have become intertwined. If we split up, I'll lose him as a roommate—and I enjoyed having him as a roommate from the very beginning.

Plus, there's Vince.

I don't want to think about that right now.

Instead, I slide my hand through Cedric's hair, in an attempt to make it behave.

It doesn't, of course.

He touches my thigh. "You know how I was hoping to start the morning? By getting a little more practice at blowjobs."

Oh, fuck.

I like hearing that word come out of his mouth.

And it's exactly what we do.

"GINNY, ELI," Michael says, bending down beside his kids. "This is Brian's friend Cedric. Can you say hello?"

"Hi, CeeCee!" Eli waves.

Ginny gives Eli an *I-can't-believe-you're-my-brother* look, which I'm well acquainted with, having two brothers of my own. She sticks out her hand and I shake it.

"Hi, *Cedric*. I'm Ginny." She's solemn, even with the goat headband. Then she says, "Are you daddies together?"

"No, we don't have any children," I tell her.

She looks at us suspiciously, and now Michael is eying us curiously, too.

"Wait a second," Michael says. "Did something happen between you two?"

Perhaps Brian and I should have discussed this in the car, but I didn't expect people to question us the minute we walked in the door, and these are Brian's friends. I'm not sure what he wants me to say, though I'm pretty sure Michael would be able to see right through any denial.

Brian, uncharacteristically, is opening and closing his mouth like a fish, no words coming out. I take a moment to appreciate how adorable this is, then say, "Uh, yes."

"Ted!" Michael shouts up the stairs. "Come down here!"

Ginny and Eli join in the shouting. "Baba!"

Ted emerges a few seconds later, looking like he was just woken up from a lovely nap by someone shrieking in his ear.

"Something happened," Ginny tells him, "but I'm not sure what."

"I made lots of treats for you." Brian holds a couple of Tupperware containers in her direction. "You like cookies, don't you?"

"Are they shaped like goats?"

"No. Does that mean you're not interested? More cookies for me and Eli?"

"No, I still want the cookies!" She jumps up and down, and Eli joins her. "What kind?"

"Can you thank Uncle Brian for bringing you cookies?" Michael asks.

"Thank you!" she sings. Then she grabs one of the containers while Brian and I take off our shoes.

In the kitchen, Ted puts a cookie on a plate for each kid. Eli breaks his cookie into at least ten pieces before eating them. Half the pieces make it into his mouth. The others…well. Ginny, on the other hand, takes bites from the whole cookie.

"Ginny," Michael says, "it was Brian's idea to go to the goat farm for your birthday, remember?"

Ginny looks like she is very fond of Brian.

I know the feeling.

"What about you?" she asks me, almost accusingly. Brian may have met her standards, but I haven't.

"I don't know anything about farms," I say apologetically. "I teach at a college and I write books."

"Do you write books about goats?"

"No, sorry."

"Then what do you write?"

"Um."

"You should write books about goats. With lots of pictures." She scurries out of the kitchen and comes back a minute later with two picture books. Both of them have "goat" in the title. "Like these ones."

"I'll think about it."

She frowns. "That's what people say when they want to say no but they're being polite. You're blowing me off."

"Ginny," Michael says.

"I will seriously consider putting goats in my next book," I tell her.

"Unicorns!" Eli shouts, crumbs falling out of his mouth.

Under the table, Brian's hand brushes my thigh, and I lose the ability to form words.

After they finish their cookies, Eli and Ginny sit at a small table in the den—within our view—and draw, while the rest of us stay in the kitchen.

Michael looks at me and Brian. "So. What happened?" He waggles his eyebrows.

"Oh, you know." Brian shrugs. "I'm irresistible and he fell for my charms."

"It's true," I say.

He looks at me and winks.

"Awww." Michael makes a heart with his fingers, the sort I've seen in K-dramas. "So, it's like that?" He turns to Brian. "You're not just fucking around, like you usually do?"

"No." Brian puts a hand on my shoulder.

Michael is doing something on his phone. FaceTime?

"Hey, Kris," he says. "You owe me twenty bucks."

"For what?" she asks.

"Brian and Cedric! I told you they'd hook up, and you didn't believe me."

"Wait a second," Brian says. "You bet on us?"

"Yup!" Michael says cheerfully. "I bet on you two, she bet against."

"I bring a guy out for drinks *one* time and—"

"Clearly I knew what I was talking about."

I turn to Ted. "How about you? What did you bet?"

"I was not a part of this," Ted says. "I do not waste money on trifling matters like *bets*."

"I didn't waste money," Michael says. "I won us twenty dollars."

Ginny rushes into the kitchen. "Is twenty dollars enough for another goat headband?" she asks Ted. "I want to get one for you, Baba!"

"Adult-sized goat headbands are very expensive," he says. "Like, two hundred bucks."

She turns to me. "Do you have two hundred bucks?"

I shake my head.

Undeterred, she goes to Brian. "Do you have two hundred bucks?"

"Uh, hello?" Kris asks from the phone. "I'm still here. Can I go back to my job now?"

"Nah, not yet," Michael says. "I wanna gloat for another five minutes."

She huffs and ends the call, which sends him into peals of laughter.

Ginny hasn't been distracted. She holds out her hand in Brian's direction.

"Ginny," Ted says, "you can't go around asking everyone for money."

"But maybe, just maybe," Michael says, "I'll get Baba a goat headband for his birthday. We can't talk about it anymore, though, because it's a *big* secret."

Satisfied, Ginny skips back to the den.

"How long has the goat phase been going on?" Brian asks.

"At least six months," Michael says. Then he holds up his arms and dances in his seat. "I won twenty dollars."

"Yeah, after you lost five bets in a row to Kris," Ted says. "We're still in the red."

Brian and I stay at Ted and Michael's for another hour, until they have to leave to take the kids to swimming lessons. In that hour, I somehow manage to become Eli's favorite person when he asks if I've seen a real unicorn and, caught off guard, I say yes. Then I have to make up stories about the unicorn for the next half hour while Brian laughs beside me on the couch.

When we're driving back home, he says, "I could not manage that full time."

"Neither could I," I agree, recalling the conversation we had about kids a couple of months ago. Talking about it now is different, now that we've been together for…

A grand total of twenty-four hours.

Twenty-four hours, and we've gone on a date and had sex and visited his friends together. Oh, and we already live together.

We lapse into silence, and I look out the window and smile. Even if the day didn't begin exactly as I'd hoped, it's been pretty damn good.

A few days later, I meet up with Spencer at our usual haunt. I'm not in the mood to keep the goofy smile off my face, so I tell him about Brian, and he's happy for me, of course.

Then he frowns. "Wait a second. You texted to ask if I knew of any apartment vacancies. I even got a lead for you. Does this mean you don't need that anymore?"

"Sorry, I should have told you earlier."

"But you were too busy doing other things?"

"Something like that."

He chuckles. "New boyfriend, and you finished your book."

"Yeah. It's going well."

"I have an idea for what we could do together next time, rather than coming here." Coffee in hand, he gestures around the room. Quiet and not-so-quiet conversations are taking place over coffee. A couple of people are studying or reading.

"Yeah?" I say. "What's that?"

"We can do in-person research for your novel. So that when you start revising it, you can make sure everything rings true, you know what I mean?"

"Is this what you do for your books?"

"They take place in space, so it's difficult. I mean, I wish I could test pilot a fusion-powered spaceship, but that's hard to pull off. Your book, on the other hand, is contemporary."

"You want us to poison someone? Or investigate a murder? I'm going to assume the latter, but I'm pretty sure such a thing would give you far too much anxiety. You'd stop sleeping, and then you'd drink more coffee to compensate. It would be a vicious cycle."

He laughs. "You know me well. No, I was thinking more along the lines of helping you make cannabis-infused dumplings."

I shudder at the thought of making dumplings. Much as I like eating them, my experience with actually making them was…not positive. My grandma attempted to give me lessons and fifteen minutes later, I was curled up in the fetal position.

Okay, that's an exaggeration.

But only a slight one. Po Po really isn't the best at teaching such things. Her instructions are unclear and her standards are high, and let me tell you, that isn't a great combination.

"I think I'll pass," I tell Spencer. "I'm happy enough consuming my weed and dumplings separately."

"But don't you want maximum verisimilitude? We can call them pot pot stickers!"

"If you're so eager to make such dumplings, you can do it yourself and report back to me. Though I'm sensing this is just an excuse to get high. You don't need an excuse—and pot brownies or muffins might be easier than dumplings."

I crack a smile as I think back to the muffin tops that I made for Brian. Yeah, that minor kitchen disaster is a fond memory for me.

Because of him.

It's been a damn long time since I felt this way about anyone.

At one point, I thought Spencer had the potential to make me feel this way, but instead, it happened with someone completely different.

[22]

BRIAN

WHEN I WAKE up the following Saturday, sunlight is streaming through the curtains, and Cedric Fong is asleep in my bed again. This time, I don't freak out, and I don't feel the need to bake enough food to feed an army. It's an improvement.

Twenty minutes later, Cedric opens his eyes and smiles at me sleepily.

"Morning," he says.

"Morning."

I reposition myself and hold him from behind.

Yes, that's right, I, Brian Poon, am spooning someone.

It really does feel good. I mean, my chest is pressed along his back, his legs are bent around mine… How could it not feel good? We're both naked except for our underwear—he refuses to sleep completely nude.

Eventually, my hand starts to wander. When I brush his nipple, he gives a little gasp, which is fuel for my libido.

Sex is a little different with him than it has been with anyone else; there are feelings involved, and sometimes that still freaks me out.

But then he rubs back against me, and oh fuck, I can't think anymore.

I slide off his boxers and fondle him. He's semi-erect, and with a few pumps, that changes. He rolls toward me, and soon we're stroking each other and kissing, and I could certainly get used to waking up like this every morning.

He cups my balls then circles his other hand around my shaft. He runs his thumb over the tip, spreading my pre-cum over the head.

Oh, *God.*

I turn him onto his stomach and drape myself over him. When he moans underneath me, I grind against him, palming his ass with one hand.

"Would you like me…to fuck you here?" I ask.

"Yeah," he groans.

Fuck. I continue to rub myself against him.

"But not today," he says hurriedly.

"No, I didn't mean today. I'll take my time and prepare you a lot beforehand."

"Mmm. Yes. Though I suspect I'm more experienced than you assume." He pauses. "My last girlfriend, five or six years ago, used to fuck me up the ass sometimes. With a strap-on."

Not what I was expecting.

And now it's my turn to groan as images pop into my head. "Was this before it ever occurred to you that you're—"

"Yeah," he says. "Why not? Straight men—or, in my case, men who assume they're straight—can like butt stuff, too."

"Some men would totally freak out at the idea of enjoying such things."

He shrugs beneath me. "I liked it. It's not something I want to do all the time, though."

I roll him over so I can kiss him properly. I feel almost overwhelmed that he trusts me with his body, that he trusts me enough to be so open with me.

My phone rings, and I jerk up as an awful realization hits me.

It must be later than I thought. I've been cocooned in bed with Cedric and forgotten about the plans I agreed to.

Vince had told Cedric that he'd be in the area this morning and wondered if he could stop by with Marissa and Lucas. Cedric asked me if that was okay, and I said yes. And my name is the one on the buzzer, the one you have to call if you want someone to open the door for you.

When I answer, sure enough, it's Vince on the other end.

I buzz him in, and then I look at Cedric. We're naked in bed together, talking about his sexual experiences, and his *brother*, my former best friend, the person who made me swear I wouldn't fool around with Cedric, is here.

I'd convinced myself it was okay. Because I care for Cedric, because I'm trying to make something work with him, but now I'm overcome with guilt.

I'm certain Vince would still not approve.

"Why aren't you getting dressed?" Cedric asks as he pulls on his boxers.

I go to my dresser and grab a shirt.

He gestures between us. "We're not telling my brother about this."

"Definitely not."

Yet the fact that he doesn't want Vince to know, even though he's unaware of my promise to Vince, makes me feel even guiltier about the whole thing.

When there's a knock on the door, I'm still not ready, but Cedric is. As I pull on some pants, I hear him hurry to the door and throw it open. There's suddenly a whole bunch of noise, and I can't help wishing it was just me and Cedric again.

I run a comb through my hair and head to the living room.

"Hey, Vince," I say, slapping him on the shoulder, "I was half-asleep when you buzzed. You know how it is after a late night."

I hope I sound natural and not like a total liar.

"Hi, Marissa. Lucas." The baby in Marissa's arms is clutching a stuffed purple dinosaur that looks well-loved. "Who's this?" I touch the dinosaur's head, and Lucas gives me a suspicious look.

"That's General Bloopy." Vince laughs. "He was actually mine when I was a kid."

"General Bloopy the Second," Cedric says. "The original General Bloopy got mowed over and Mom had to replace him. Vince didn't know the truth until last year." He punches his brother's shoulder. "He thought General Bloopy went to the spa for a week and came back looking newer."

I can't help noticing Cedric's ease with Vince. How their relationship is nothing like mine and my brother's. Of course, my brother and I didn't grow up together and he's more than a decade older than me, whereas Vince and Cedric are only two years apart. So, it never would have been quite the same, but still.

I'm a bit envious, and then there's the guilt. Back in the day, Vince often knew who I was fucking; I didn't always tell him, but I didn't try to keep such things a secret from him. And, I'm not gonna lie, I also enjoyed watching him with women on occasion.

Now, I'm fucking his brother.

Jesus.

"Brian?" Vince peers at me. "Are you okay?"

"Of course," I say, perhaps a little too cheerfully, "but we haven't had our morning coffee yet. Would you like some coffee?"

"Sounds good," Marissa says. "This little guy kept me up half the night."

Lucas smiles mischievously in response.

Vince gives me an odd look. "*We* haven't had our morning coffee yet? Do you always have your coffee together?"

Cedric shrugs. "Usually, yeah. Sometimes he bakes for me, too."

"You *bake*?" Vince asks. "Since when? What do you bake?"

I gesture grandly at a Tupperware on the kitchen island, and soon, we're all drinking coffee and eating biscotti around the dining room table.

Everyone except for Lucas, that is, but it's not for lack of trying. He's quite grabby these days. Vince pretends to make General Bloopy—how on earth did the dinosaur get that name?—loudly eat biscotti, similar to how Cookie Monster sounds when he eats cookies, and Lucas giggles.

I glance at Cedric, who's dipping his biscotti into his coffee, and I'm suddenly very turned on by his large hands. They feel really good when they're running over my back or cupping my face so he can kiss me…

I can't think such things right now.

Vince passes Lucas to Cedric, and Lucas immediately springs into action. He grabs Cedric's biscotti and drops it on the floor, looking quite proud of himself.

"Don't worry," I say to Cedric. "Lots more biscotti, plus your favorite muffins."

"His favorite," Vince murmurs.

It sounds suspicious to my ears, and once again, I feel guilty.

"Wow, you really have gotten into baking," Marissa says. "Can you make a matcha double fromage cheesecake?"

"Don't worry." Vince plants a quick kiss on her cheek. "We'll pick one up from Cheese & Me while we're down here."

I want to look at Cedric again, but I'm afraid someone—maybe Lucas—will notice the way I'm looking at him and start asking questions.

Holding Lucas solidly around the waist, Cedric stands the baby up on his feet, facing toward Cedric. Lucas grabs his uncle's nose and starts twisting. Not hard, but Cedric pretends otherwise.

"Ahhh," Cedric says, which only spurs Lucas to start twisting more.

Vince grips Lucas's hand. "Now, we went over this yesterday. You don't grab people's noses and twist. It's hurty."

I can't help laughing.

"Vince's mother says Lucas is just like him." Marissa smiles. "He's almost crawling. He's sort of figured out how to move backward, but he can't go forward yet. When he does, I'm sure he'll be so much trouble. Just like you." She ruffles Vince's hair.

Vince and Marissa don't stay for too long—apparently Lucas has a strict schedule that he needs to adhere to, or he gets cranky —but although their visit is less than an hour, it feels way longer.

I'm immensely relieved when I shut the door behind them. I lean back on the door, tip my head up, and close my eyes.

Only for a moment, though.

Because now it's just Cedric and me, and I can look at him without worrying about raising anyone's suspicions. When I kiss him, he tastes like coffee and my baking, and something that's just *him*.

"Seeing Vince was awkward," he says.

"You seemed perfectly normal the whole time," I tell him.

"I did? I sure didn't feel like it." He pauses. "We probably should have talked about this before, but... I'd prefer to wait a little while before telling my family. So, if we could continue to pretend we're just roommates, that would be best."

That's what I want, too. I don't want to deal with it yet.

But I'm still a little hurt that Cedric doesn't want his family to know. He's pretty close to his family, after all. How often does he keep secrets like this from them?

Does this mean he's struggling to believe our relationship can last? Because I'm so inexperienced with such things?

I open my mouth to ask him, then close it.

I'm not sure I want to know the answer.

Instead, I slide my hands down to his ass and grab a generous handful of it. I'll distract myself with sex, as I've done many times before.

It's one of the few things I'm good at.

[23]
CEDRIC

AFTER A BREAK OF A FEW WEEKS, I'm working on my book again. The first thing I do is read the whole thing over and figure out what I need to fix.

The answer?

A lot.

I'm wildly repetitive, but there are also massive inconsistencies, and some things just plain don't make sense. Though it's overwhelming, I start my revisions, beginning with the big changes I need to make.

In some ways, things are back to how they were before I finished the first draft, before Brian and I kissed.

And in other ways, not at all.

I do three hours of work every weekday morning, and he never bothers me during those hours. He still prepares my breakfast and makes coffee for me.

But he always kisses me before I go to the office to work.

And I wake up in his bed every morning.

In fact, I hardly use my bedroom at all, except as a place to keep my clothes.

I've never lived with a partner before, let alone started dating while we're roommates, and though I like it, it's a little weird at times. It's hard to take things slowly when living together, and a part of me feels like this is moving a bit too fast.

Some nights, Brian goes out without me. He always asks if I want to come, but I rarely do. I don't like going out and meeting new people as much as he does.

And although he kissed me after I told him that he should be an event planner, to my knowledge, he hasn't started looking into it, nor has he asked to talk to Naomi, which I'd offered to set up for him.

The first Friday afternoon in June, I'm working on my book when Brian knocks on the office door and enters with a cup of tea for me.

"Thank you," I say.

I'm glad for the distraction. I'm stuck on my portrayal of Mrs. Tom, my main character's nemesis, who is *not* the killer of the bakery owner, by the way. Her character is the most inconsistent thing in my manuscript.

Is there sexual tension between her and the protagonist while they're arguing about their grandchildren? Hmm.

"Let's go out for dinner tonight," I say to Brian, "and this time, how about I pick the place? You don't have to plan all our dates." I grab his hand and pull him closer to me.

"Sure." He bends down to kiss me. "Where are we going?"

"You'll see. Now quit distracting me."

He laughs when I swat his ass.

We head out for dinner around seven, and as we approach Chinatown, I start to worry. I'm not sure if Brian will appreciate a hole-in-the-wall restaurant.

But when we get our food—I tell him to order the shrimp wonton noodle soup—and he tastes it, I wonder why I worried. If the food is good, Brian will enjoy it, even if it's not as fancy as the places he usually frequents.

This restaurant has been here for fifty years, owned by a

family that came to Canada a bit after my mother's family. I recognize the server, whom I think is one of the granddaughters, but I can't recall her name.

Brian wouldn't have forgotten. He knows people everywhere he goes, and he's good with names and faces. I'm always impressed by that.

"In my book," I say, "there's a restaurant similar to this one. That's why I wanted to come here tonight."

Afterward, we go to a bakery that's much like the bakery my grandparents used to run. He gets a pineapple bun and I get a cocktail bun, which we eat as we walk along Baldwin Street, heading to our destination for drinks.

At Lychee, we manage to snag the same table we sat at back in February. Brian orders the drink that comes in the lightbulb, and I order the bear's head one, just because. When it arrives, it looks as fantastic as I remember, and I snap a picture.

He gestures between us. "How about we take a picture for Instagram?"

Most of Brian's pictures are of food and drinks and the places he goes, plus a few selfies. He occasionally posts pictures of himself with his friends, but not often. If he's suggesting we take a photo of the two of us, it would feel like he's claiming me.

And I like that, but I'm not quite ready for such a public declaration of our relationship. After all, he has ten thousand followers.

"Some other time," I tell him. "I mean, Vince might see."

"You're right."

There's an uncomfortable beat of silence, but then I glance at my drink and grin. "Remember that first night we came here? I'd seen you before, but Valentine's was the first day we actually spent any time together."

He nods. "I thought you were cute."

"Did you?"

"And I liked the way you laughed when this cocktail arrived."

He gestures at my glass. "Plus, you were wasted, and you were all over me."

"I was not *all* over you."

"You didn't realize you're an affectionate drunk?"

"Yes, I know that, but saying I was all over you is an exaggeration."

He gives me an *I'm-humoring-you* smile, which ought to piss me off, but it doesn't.

"You must not have minded too much," I say, "because that was the day you asked if I wanted to live with you."

His expression turns more intense and serious than usual—a look I don't see when he's with anyone but me, and I can't deny it thrills me a little.

"I'm very glad I asked you," he says softly.

I shiver at his words.

The way the fancy lights in here illuminate his face…it makes him look particularly handsome, and I wish I could paint him like this.

Alas, that's not one of my talents. I write instead, and my main character is a seventy-five-year-old grandma, but that doesn't mean she isn't getting a romance in my series. Something is hinted at between her and the scandalously young owner of a fruit and vegetable mart—he's sixty-five—but I don't think it's working.

Then all of a sudden, I have it.

Her love interest should be Mrs. Tom. My elderly grandmother isn't going to be straight.

"Cedric?" Brian squeezes my leg.

"I figured something out for my book," I say. "I need to get home."

As I start guzzling my Wild Beary cocktail, I feel a touch guilty. I'm supposed to be on a date with Brian.

"I'm sorry. I—"

He waves this off. "It's fine. I like when you get excited about things. Besides, we've already had dinner and dessert and a drink."

"I'll make it up to you, I promise." I wink at him.

It's an easy walking distance, but we take a cab because it's faster. Though, given the traffic, not by much.

As soon as we arrive home, I go to the office and scribble a few things in my notebook—with any luck, I'll actually be able to read them later—then pull up the manuscript on my computer and start making changes.

Brian enters a few minutes later with a mug of rooibos.

"Don't stay up too late," he says.

"I won't."

I'm not sure I mean it.

At three in the morning, after more than four hours of working on my manuscript, I've finished changing Mrs. Tom's scenes—and adding a couple of new ones. I haven't had a burst of inspiration quite like that in years, and it's exhilarating. I'm thankful Brian allowed me to have this without complaint.

When I'm ready for sleep, I walk to his bedroom, then realize that climbing into bed next to Brian might wake him. Better to sleep in my own bed—for the first time in weeks—instead.

It's weird lying in my bed again without a warm body next to me. Without *him*.

Although I'm tired, my brain is still active, and I grab my phone from the bedside table when I have an idea. Not a writing idea this time.

No, an idea for Brian.

You can order basically anything on the internet these days. I can't find exactly what I'm looking for, but I do find the next best thing.

~

I awake at eight, feeling refreshed even though I've only had four hours of sleep, and I know what I want to do this morning. I head to the washroom to shower and prepare myself, then I tiptoe into Brian's room and climb into bed.

He slings an arm over me.

"Hey." His voice is rough with sleep. "You do everything you wanted last night?"

"Not quite."

I curl my body around his, and he immediately notices that I'm naked. A moment later, he's on top of me, kissing me hard, his hands roaming my body. Over my stomach, my hip, my thigh, but not between my legs.

When he cups my cheeks, his tenderness makes me gasp.

"I want you," I tell him.

"I know." And that's when he finally grasps my erection.

I inhale swiftly at his touch, and then I start stroking him, too.

When he swears under his breath, it gives me such a rush. I roll onto my stomach, grab his hand, and put it on my ass. "I want you to fuck me today. Here."

"You sure?" he asks, stroking his hand over me.

"Yeah. I'm sure."

"I want to lick you first. Is that okay?"

I nod, and when his tongue makes contact with my taint, I shiver. We haven't done this before, and I'm so sensitive there. And then he swirls his tongue around my opening.

He grabs some lube before he returns to rimming me, and I squirm against his mouth. His lubed-up finger slides along my crack before entering me, and I hiss out a breath. He reaches around to stroke me with his other hand.

God, it's all so overwhelming.

When I start to turn around, he removes his hands from my body.

It's not that I wasn't enjoying myself, but there's something else I want to do, too. He's on his knees, and that's perfect. I bend over and circle my tongue over the head of his penis, then take more of it in my mouth. I like to think I've gotten pretty good at this in the past few weeks, and based on the sounds he's making, I'm not wrong.

He runs his hand through my hair. "You're going to have to stop that soon if you want…"

I raise my head.

Yes, I want.

"How would you like to do it?" he asks.

I roll onto my back, spread my legs, and bend my knees up. For some reason, it's important to see his face when he slides inside me.

He squeezes more lube on his fingers and works two of them into my ass.

"You're gonna feel so good," he murmurs.

When he rolls on a condom and lubes himself up, my heart is beating quickly in anticipation. He rubs the tip of his cock over me and slowly starts pushing inside.

"Okay?" he asks.

"Yes."

He goes in a little farther. "How's that?"

I breathe in sharply and try to bear down. I haven't done this in a while.

"You can do it." He runs his hand over my cheek and through my hair, and I can't help feeling like I'm incredibly special to him.

He leisurely kisses my neck for a minute before pushing his cock farther inside, watching my face the whole time. I like that I can take it. I think he's all the way in me now.

Nope, I was wrong. One last push.

"There." The word is almost strangled, like this is too intense for him to speak properly.

And then he starts moving inside me.

I hold him against me with one arm, and with the other hand, I grip the sheets.

"Too much?" he asks.

"Yes, but don't stop." My words come out in a rush.

He grins at me, that cocky grin I love, but then it changes to something more beautiful. And searing. Perhaps it's foolish of me, but I doubt he's ever looked at anyone else like this before.

He strokes my cock, and I'm practically thrashing beneath him…

I grip the sheets tightly as I come, spurting onto his hand and my stomach, and he shudders inside me and finds his own release.

After we clean up, we hold each other for a long time. I fall asleep with my arms around him, my lack of sleep the night before finally catching up to me, and when I awake, he's setting down a tray with warm muffins and mugs of coffee.

I don't think most people could possibly imagine how sweet he is with me.

～

Several days later, a package arrives. Fortunately, it happens in the morning, when Brian is out. I immediately wrap it in the silver paper and red bow I bought the other day, and when he returns home, I give it to him.

"For me?" he asks, sounding surprised.

"Don't look so thrilled when you don't even know what it is. Maybe you won't like it." My tone is light, but inside, there's a strange pressure in my chest.

How often do people give him gifts? I get the sense that it's a rare occurrence.

He tears open the paper, revealing a box containing four lightbulb drinking glasses.

"What an *illuminating* gift." He doesn't make terrible jokes around everyone. Just me.

After the bad pun, he smiles at me fondly and kisses me on the lips.

Something can happen over and over again, and then suddenly—on the twentieth, forty-third, or eighty-fifth time—feel completely different than it ever did before.

It's a Wednesday morning, and I head to the kitchen for breakfast.

"Good morning." Brian hands me a mug of coffee, just the way I like it, as he's done so many times in the past few months.

And I realize that I love him.

It just whooshes over me.

But knowing it and feeling ready to say it are two different things.

I'm quieter than usual as I eat and take my second cup of coffee to the office. I'm deep in revisions, and there's lots I'd planned to do today, but instead, I walk over to the window and sip my coffee as I stare out at the streets.

I'm not afraid of love, but by thirty-six, I suspect many people have been badly burned or betrayed in relationships, and I'm no exception. So, as well as it's going with Brian, I no longer jump in with both feet quite the way I did when I was twenty and had my first girlfriend. Each time, I'm a little more cautious.

It's been a while since I felt like this, and I know it'll take a bit longer before I'm completely comfortable with these feelings. Before I'm able to tell him.

And before he's ready to hear it, for that matter.

Because I don't think he is, not yet.

I scrub a hand over my face before sitting down at my computer and working on somebody else's romance rather than my own.

[24]

BRIAN

IN THE PAST FEW DAYS, Cedric has spent more time in his office than usual, and he goes on more frequent head-clearing walks, which he says he'd prefer to do alone. He still sleeps in my bed, and we still eat meals together, but I have a feeling that something is off.

Is he avoiding me?

God, I'm a mess when it comes to these things.

But I take comfort in the lightbulb glasses, of all things. A present that was clearly bought specifically for me, that reminds me of our non-Valentine's date.

And I take comfort in the fact that when we're in bed, it still feels different than it did with anyone else.

One evening, just before nine, I knock on the office door and open it a crack.

"I'm meeting Elsie for a drink soon," I say. "You coming?" He'd said he might.

"Oh, right." He drags his gaze away from the books open on his desk; he likely has about sixteen tabs open in his browser, too. "I'm really sorry, but I'm in the middle of something." He comes over and wraps his arms around me. "This is a nice shirt. Ashton Chang again?"

"Ascot Chang."

"Right, right." He's a little absent right now, lost in his work. "Have fun. I'll join you some other time, or if I get stuck, maybe I'll text you and come out later."

I nod, because I'm the supportive boyfriend who wants him to work on his book. It's important to him, and it's not like he isn't spending time with me.

But I can't stop myself from feeling a little disappointed.

Maybe he picks up on it, because he pulls me closer and gives me a long goodbye kiss.

I meet Elsie for a drink, as planned, but it's hard to focus on what she's saying. I keep having to ask her to repeat herself, and I feel bad about that, but my brain just isn't working the way it usually does.

"Brian?" Elsie says. "Are you okay? You seem a little quiet today."

I shoot her a reassuring smile. "Don't worry about me. I'm good. As always."

She hesitates, as though deciding whether to accept this answer, then says, "I have a question for you." She sips her drink. "Any recommendations for where I should host my birthday gathering this year?"

As I answer her, I think about what Cedric told me. About how I'm good at this, how I always have ideas. Nobody had ever said that to me, but people do tend to ask me for recommendations like this, it's true. I *am* good at it.

When I get home, it's eleven thirty. I don't have the desire to stay out as late these days, now that I have someone to come home to. Someone who just happens to be reading in my bed.

Shirtless.

When Cedric sees me, he smiles and sets his book aside. "How was it?"

"Good."

There's a minute of silence as I undress and climb into bed. He embraces me and kisses me, and I feel all my doubts, all my fears that he was pulling away and there was some kind of distance growing between us—I feel them fade away.

Touching him can be magic, and I'm lucky I go to sleep beside him each night.

I know that soon enough, those uncertainties will be back, but for now…

[25]

CEDRIC

WE HAVEN'T HAD a family dinner in a month, and a lot has changed for me in that time.

My mother hands me the bok choy. "You're not teaching the spring/summer term, right?"

"That's right," I say. "More time for writing." *And fucking.*

"Did you finish the first draft?" Courtney asks.

"Yes. I'm revising it now."

Po Po sniffs. "I still don't know much about this book. You say there is murder and poison, but what else? I do not believe it actually exists. You are just talking shit!"

"Po Po!" Julian says. "I don't want Evie to repeat those words."

She ignores him and keeps talking to me. "I think you are too embarrassed to admit you aren't writing, so you are pretending. But don't worry, I am here to give you ideas. You could have talking dinosaurs?" She gestures at General Bloopy, who is sitting in his own chair beside Evie's high chair.

"A purple talking dinosaur," I say. "Geez, what an original idea."

"I think you are laughing at me."

"Po Po, I promise I'm writing a book, okay?"

"Did you try out any poison on Brian?"

"No…"

"I still don't like you living with him. I bet he is encouraging you to lie to your po po about this book."

Vince starts laughing his head off, and Lucas and Evie join him.

"I'm not lying!" My cheeks heat. "Mom, you believe me, don't you?"

"Yeah, sure, honey."

My mother doesn't sound convincing, and I'm not sure if she's just trying to mess with me.

I feel very off-kilter.

"So, what else is new with you, Cedric?" Dad asks.

Why is everyone focusing on me today? Can they tell that something big is up?

I look around the table, at my parents, my grandma, my brothers, and their wives, and I consider telling them about Brian. But I just…I can't.

Fuck it, I'll talk about the book and get it over with. I'll have to do it at some point anyway.

"My novel," I say. "It's a cozy mystery—"

"What is a cozy mystery?" Po Po interrupts. "This sounds like a made-up thing. Are you saying dead bodies are cozy?"

"—about a Chinese grandma who has started selling her special dumplings to put her granddaughter through med school—"

"This was my idea! You are really using it! Is there marijuana in the dumplings?"

"There is. And when she makes her first delivery, she finds a dead body. The owner of her favorite bakery in Chinatown. She immediately suspects Mrs. Tom, whose son runs the rival bakery…"

"This sounds like a lot of fun, Cedric," Mom says.

"This is a book about me!" Po Po shouts. "I am Chinese grandmother, I make amazing dumplings. Now I'm going to be in my own book. Will be famous!"

"The main character isn't *you*," I say, "but yes, you are some of the inspiration. She's more than ten years younger than you, though."

"That is for the best! I could run much better when I was only eighty. Better for escaping bad guys."

"In cozy mysteries, there isn't usually much…"

I trail off as my grandmother gets up from her chair.

"Ma!" Mom says. "Are you trying to run?"

"Yes, I am curious to see how well I can run now."

Julian stands up and helps her back into her seat. "If you fall, you could get very hurt."

She sniffs but stays sitting.

"You will dedicate your book to me, Cedric," she says, "and take me all over the world on your book tour, yes?"

"Uh, Po Po," I say, "it's unlikely I will go on some big international book tour. And a publisher still has to buy the book."

"I will write to the editors."

"No! That's not how it's done. It's my agent's job, and I won't give her the book until I've done more revisions." Spencer enjoys self-publishing, but I don't think that's for me.

"Okay, then I will make you another two hundred dumplings so you don't have to cook and can focus on writing."

"How come he gets more dumplings?" Vince asks. "That's not fair."

"You write book about me, then we talk."

"He also got dumplings for being in the bachelor auction."

"Well, you are married. Not like you could have done it. Would you rather have smart, pretty wife and baby, or bachelor auction and two hundred dumplings?"

"I—"

"Exactly, you take wife and baby."

There's something else about the book that I should probably mention.

"It's going to be a whole series, I hope."

"This is good news!" Po Po says. "A whole series about me."

"And throughout the series, the main character and Mrs. Tom have…a romance."

"Wait, she has romance with murderer? Oh, I get it. Mrs. Tom is not murderer. That would be too obvious."

I wait for her to realize the rest.

"She is having romance with another woman?" Po Po asks.

"Yes."

I wait anxiously, unable to swallow my noodles. I tell myself it'll be okay, no matter what happens. I'll go home to Brian, and he'll support my work no matter what.

"Is she hot?" Po Po asks at last.

I frown. "What?"

"Mrs. Tom. Is she hot?

"Um." I'm baffled by the trajectory of this conversation. "Well, she's seventy-two—"

"You are saying old people cannot be sexy?"

"No, it's just…*I'm* not attracted to people who are almost forty years older than me—"

"I give you extra dumplings if you make her very sexy. Like Michelle Yeoh, maybe?"

"Michelle Yeoh isn't that old—" Julian begins.

"He gets even *more* dumplings?" Vince is outraged, and I can't help laughing.

"Only if he follows my demands." Po Po lifts her nose in the air.

"You're not allowed to make demands," I tell her. "Like I said, this character isn't you. There are lots of Chinese grandmothers who make good dumplings—"

"Wah, what are you saying? My dumplings are not special?"

"No, of course not, but you don't use cannabis and you're not busy solving crimes—"

"How do you know?"

"But I will dedicate it to you, yes."

Po Po stops all her questioning and stands up so she can give me a big hug.

The drive back home—Brian has allowed me to borrow his car—takes far too long. I'm impatient to tell him what happened.

Indeed, he laughs at my family's antics as we sip our drinks in the living room.

"What possessed you to tell your family about your book?" he asks.

I shrug. "I was too nervous to tell them about you. This seemed easier."

He stiffens—no, that's probably just my imagination.

Still, I kiss him to show that I do care about him, very much, even if I'm not quite ready to say "I love you" yet.

But I think I will be ready soon.

[26]

BRIAN

"LAST I CHECKED," Carrie says, swirling her drink as she sits on my couch, "this is not the classic glass in which one serves a Manhattan."

Carrie Lo came over to my place after work. She's wearing a pencil skirt and a blouse, and her hair is pulled up in a chignon.

"Does it not meet your standards?" I ask.

"It's just an interesting choice."

"Cedric bought them."

I immediately realize my mistake. Man, I'm really off my game today.

"Cedric?" she says. "Cedric Fong?"

"Yeah, he needed a place to live, so I invited him to live with me."

"And he got you lightbulb glasses."

"Mm-hmm."

"You seem quite fond of them."

She gives me a searching look, and I find myself smiling.

"Did he move in before or after you started fucking him?" she asks.

"It's not like what you're imagining."

"What *am* I imagining?"

"I don't know," I say. "That it started as something sexual?"

"So, you became friends first and then fell in love?"

"I—"

"OMG this is so exciting!" she shrieks. "It's so unlike you. And it's all thanks to me."

"What on earth are you talking about?"

"You didn't really know him before the bachelor auction, right? I encouraged you to bid on a date with him."

"You did not," I protest, then have a long sip of my cocktail.

"Yes, I did!"

"No, you just said 'that poor girl' when the woman's mom was bidding on her behalf. That's all."

"Well, it spurred you on," she says.

"You're taking entirely too much credit for this."

"I introduced Vince and Marissa, too!"

"I thought you just told Marissa who Vince was when she laid eyes on him."

"Same difference." She laughs.

"But you can't tell Vince or Marissa about me and Cedric."

"Why not?"

"Because I promised Vince that nothing would happen between me and his brother."

Carrie rubs her hands together, excited by all this drama. "That's because Vince thought you'd fuck Cedric a couple of times and break his heart. But now you're in love." She grins. "I knew it would happen eventually. This explains why you were acting weird the night we went out with Holden."

"That was before anything happened with Cedric. But I was still having trouble thinking of anyone else."

"You're so cute."

I'm torn between feeling exasperated and pleased. Carrie is happy for me, and she didn't immediately tell me I'd fuck this up, which is nice.

"Are you sure I can't tell Vince?" she asks. "I'm going to see him and Marissa tomorrow. I'm babysitting so they can go on a date, and I bought this cute little outfit for Lucas. What do you think?" She pulls up a picture on her phone.

"I don't think it'll stay clean for long. Lucas doesn't take care of his clothes like I do."

She slaps my shoulder. "You can't hide this from Vince forever. Does Cedric know about your promise?"

I shake my head. "But he still has no interest in telling his family. Though he does know I had a crush on Vince."

"And it bothers you that he doesn't want to tell them. Like you're a dirty secret."

"Yeah, like he doesn't believe it can last. Because I'm, you know."

"Brian, don't be so glum! Think about Vince, for example. He was just like you, didn't want anything serious, and now he's happily married. Some people don't really do relationships until they find the right person, that's all. And you're a very caring guy."

"You think that?"

"Of course! I understand why he wouldn't tell his family yet. Do you think I've told my family about everyone I've dated? No! His family makes a big deal out of things. I get it."

"As if you don't make a big deal out of things," I mutter.

God, this really has me twisted inside out. I'm not usually so damn insecure.

I just can't shake the feeling that something isn't quite right, and that Cedric would normally tell his family—his brothers, if not his parents and grandma—about someone he'd been dating for a month. I mean, if my family were cool with me dating someone of any gender, I'd let them know right away.

"Has he told anyone about the two of you?" she asks.

"He mentioned telling a friend." It's not like he's kept me a complete secret, that's true. "You can see Cedric and me as a couple?"

"I don't know Cedric very well," Carrie says, "but yes! I think you make sense together."

I sip my drink. "He told me I should be an event planner. Do you think—"

"You'd be fantastic. What, you don't think so? Or are you worried he just said it because you're sleeping together?"

"That's what led to us kissing for the first time. When he told me that."

"You two really are cute. Are you considering getting a job?"

"I'd like to work, but I haven't looked into it yet. I'm just focused on my relationship."

"Before I forget." Carrie waves her drink around, and I'm half-afraid she's going to break the lightbulb glass. "Sam Leung is having a party. Last Saturday of the month. You and Cedric should come. Bring another friend, if you like. Sam won't mind—friends of friends are always invited."

Once, I would have been one of the first people to know about Sam Leung's parties. His house wasn't far from mine. Not on the Bridle Path, but one of the nearby streets.

If you show up at one of his parties, there's a good chance you won't see him, though. He's a mysterious, eccentric man who tends to keep to himself, so why he throws a couple of big parties a year, I have no idea.

I haven't been to something like this for a while. It sounds fun. Perhaps Kris, Ted, or Michael would like to come, too. I'll ask.

When Carrie leaves, it's seven o'clock. Cedric was meeting some friends earlier, and he should be back any minute. Dammit.

Not because I don't want to see him, but because I still need to finish frosting the cake that I made for him earlier.

I'm halfway through when the door starts to open. I scurry over to meet Cedric, and as soon as he closes the door behind him, I cover his eyes with one hand.

"What's this about?" he asks.

"I'm doing something for you, but you can't see yet. Take off your shoes and go straight to your room until I tell you to come out."

"You're making it sound like I did something naughty."

"Maybe you did." I smack his ass. "If I remove my hand, will you promise to close your eyes?"

He nods, and I bend down to remove his shoes. Then I lead him to his room, enjoying the feel of his hand in mine.

"Alright, here you are," I say when we're in his bedroom. "You can open your eyes."

He immediately tries to sneak under my arm and make a run for the door.

I laugh and push him onto the bed; he goes easily. He's strong enough to stop me if he wanted to, but he doesn't.

I straddle him, and we kiss. He slips his hand under my shirt…

"No," I say. "I gotta work on your surprise. It'll be ready in fifteen minutes."

I return to the kitchen, where I finish putting buttercream on the sides of the cake. Then I make chocolate curls with a vegetable peeler and use those to decorate the top of the cake.

"You can come out now!" I call down the hall.

Cedric walks into the kitchen. "Wow. You made that?"

"Chocolate fudge cake with praline buttercream." I gesture toward it with a flourish.

"It looks like it came from a bakery. What's the occasion?"

"Just wanted to do something nice for you."

He gives me a strange look. "You don't need to. The breakfasts every morning—that's already a lot."

I don't understand. I made him a cake. What's wrong with that? Am I screwing up this relationship business again? And is he avoiding me at times, or am I just imagining it?

I must be showing all of my vulnerability, because he wraps his arm around me.

"I like it," he says. "I just don't want you to feel it's necessary to do lots of big things for me. I'll like you no matter what, okay?"

I exhale. That does make me feel a bit better, but being over the top is just who I am. He's saying I don't need to be myself?

He picks up a knife, and that snaps me out of my thoughts.

"No, you can't eat it yet," I say. "Dinner first."

"Since when are you such a stickler for propriety?" He chuckles. "Do you have anything planned for dinner, or should I make something?"

I pull two items out of the cupboard and set them on the kitchen island.

"My favorite noodles!" he says. "They'd run out the last time I went to H-Mart."

And they were still out yesterday, but I have my ways.

We eat the noodles, and then he slices the cake. I'm pleased to see that all three layers, as well as the buttercream in between, are perfectly even.

Although the cake is as delicious as I'd hoped, I can't fully enjoy it. Cedric might care for me and understand me better than most people, but he still thinks I'm a little much.

I push those thoughts aside. "You want to go to Sam Leung's party in a couple of weeks? You know, the guy who lives near the Bridle Path and has a better hedge maze than I did?"

"I've never met him."

"You might not meet him at the party, either, but do you want to come?"

"Sure," he says. "Not quite my scene, but it could be fun."

He squeezes my hand and smiles at me, and though I smile back, it feels just a bit forced.

[27]

CEDRIC

BRIAN ARRANGES A CAR SERVICE, and we pull up to Sam Leung's mansion at about nine. The two of us, plus Carrie and Kris. Ted and Michael couldn't come—and frankly, I don't think Ted would have wanted to come anyway—but Kris was curious to see how "rich fuckers" lived. Plus, she wanted an excuse to avoid an uncomfortable family dinner.

I always feel a little out of place around this sort of wealth. My family is well-off, no question, but my parents aren't as showy about it, and then…there's me. The one who went into the arts and never made a fortune, unlike Vince and Julian.

But Brian's here, and he belongs—and he looks particularly sharp in a pinstripe suit. Carrie is wearing a sequin-covered dress, and Kris is in a well-fitted suit, with vest and bowtie. Her hair has recently been dyed bright pink. I thought I saw Carrie checking Kris out earlier, but maybe that was my imagination.

Near the fountain, the four of us get out of the car and head inside the house. A couple of people I don't know immediately appear and hug Brian.

"Hey," one of them says. "What happened to you? Haven't seen you in ages."

A man in a shiny suit is giving air kisses to Carrie. Music that I'm not cool enough to know is playing in the background.

Maybe this was a mistake.

It's weird seeing Brian in another part of his life. I'm more used to the side of him that makes me breakfast and brings me tea when I'm working late.

I don't know Kris all that well, but the two of us stick together as people greet Brian and push drinks into his hand. I soon lose track of him; there are lots of people and it's a big house.

Kris and I don't talk much, other than her muttering "what the fuck" and "what the hell is that" as we wander around. She asks for a beer from the bartender—I think she's the only one drinking beer here—and I get some wine.

"Cedric Fong!" says a man as he approaches me. It takes me a moment to place him.

Alvin from the bachelor auction.

He slaps my shoulder as if we're old friends. "When's your next book coming out? You writing anything these days?"

This topic of conversation doesn't bother me quite as much as it used to. It no longer reminds me that I *can't* write.

"I'm working on something a little different," I tell him.

"A screenplay?"

I chuckle. "No, it's a novel, but a different genre."

Alvin isn't as nosy as my grandma, thankfully.

I spend the next hour talking to a few people around the edges of the party. At one point, I think I see Sam Leung, but he quickly disappears, and I almost wonder if I saw a ghost instead.

I consider adding a reclusive rich man like Sam to my series, and I laugh at the thought of my main character and Mrs. Tom trying to break into his house, though I probably shouldn't laugh about such a crime.

After making a quick note on my phone, I wander out to the gardens to look for Brian, but he's nowhere to be found.

The party is okay, yet I'm most excited about going home

with him, discussing the evening, and finding out what he knows about Sam—Brian often knows things that nobody else knows. I probably won't be in the mood for sex if we get home well after midnight, but tomorrow morning…

I'm feeling pretty good about my life these days. I have a boyfriend—and I'm getting used to how strong my feelings are for him. I'm also writing, and I'll soon be in possession of more dumplings from my grandmother.

"Hey, Cedric?"

Lost in my own world, I startle at the voice. When I turn around, I see another familiar face from the bachelor auction.

"Kelvin Kwong?" I say, his name coming out as a question even though I'm pretty sure it's him. When someone is both a doctor and an astronaut, you tend not to forget them.

"It's a nice night out. Enjoying a little peace and quiet away from the cacophony in there?" He gestures toward the house.

For some reason, I feel the desire to make inane space jokes, but he's probably heard them all before, so I stop myself and fumble for another topic. "How was your Valentine's date?"

"Not bad," he says, "but her family was a bit much, if you know what I mean."

He seems surprisingly ordinary for a guy with his level of achievement.

"Are you going to participate again next year?" I ask.

"If they want me, sure. It's for a good cause, after all. And you?"

Well, this is a bit awkward.

"If I'm single…" Which I hopefully won't be. I glance around, but I don't see Brian in the gardens. "And if my family bribes me again, but they'll have to up their game. Two hundred dumplings won't be enough."

Kelvin laughs and steps toward me.

"You want to see the hedge maze?" he asks. "I've heard it's a quality one."

[28]

BRIAN

I STAND OUTSIDE the back doors. The backyard is on a slope, and I look downward, to where Cedric and Kelvin fucking Kwong are talking by the rose bushes. In the right light, Cedric's hair has a reddish-brown sheen, as it does now.

I clutch my glass in my right hand. A goddamn astronaut is hitting on my boyfriend.

And now they're moving in the direction of the hedge maze...

Oh, hell no.

I place my drink on a table and hurry down the slope. I'm practically sprinting, and I can feel people giving me strange looks, but I don't give a damn.

I grab Cedric's elbow. "You need to come with me. *Now.*"

"What's wrong?" He looks perplexed.

I pull him behind a bush, and Kelvin doesn't follow us. Good.

"He's hitting on you," I hiss, "and I can't stand it any longer."

"What?" Cedric says. "We were just having a conversation."

"He asked you to go to the hedge maze, didn't he? That's a code."

"A code? But there's an actual hedge maze here. I've never

seen one before, and I'm curious. Could be something I put in my book—"

"That's where people go to make out!"

"Oh." Cedric's eyes widen.

"And his body language… It was obvious."

"Have you been watching me the whole time? I don't need babysitting, and if he wanted to kiss me, you know I wouldn't have been interested, and I'm sure I could have handled the situation. But I thought he was straight—"

"Because his biography at the bachelor auction said he was only interested in women? You think everyone would tell the truth at a place like that? You did, sure, but not everyone's family is like yours. Your family doesn't just barely tolerate you; they accept you. Yet you won't tell them about us."

He peers at me. "Is that what this is about?"

"And you seem to be avoiding me, not just tonight."

"What are you talking about? We spend tons of time together. We *live* together."

"And you told me I shouldn't bake fancy cakes for you."

"I don't want you to feel like you always need to make big gestures. That's all."

"But that's who I am!" I say. "I do shit like that!"

His face softens. "I know. I'm sorry. Maybe I felt guilty because you were putting more effort into such things, and I just took five minutes to order you lightbulb glasses. And bought you chocolate, but that was before we were even dating. I won't say that anymore, okay? But I do think… Have you even looked into event planning?"

"No! Because you're the most important part of my life. I want to focus on that first, and even still, I seem to be failing at it."

"You're not, I promise."

I don't know who I am right now. It's not like me to freak out like this.

"I've never had a relationship before," I say. "I don't know what I'm doing."

"Okay, back up. First of all, I'm not avoiding you, but I like having my own space sometimes. Yes, I've spent a lot of time on my writing lately because I'm not teaching and I actually have something I want to write for once. But it's about forty hours a week—a job. It's not unreasonable, and you know it's important to me."

Right, I'm the loser who doesn't understand this shit because I don't have a career.

He takes my hand, and I let him. He's managing to be reasonably calm, and when he touches me, I feel a little of his calmness seeping into my pores.

"Having our own lives is healthy," he says, "and you don't have to focus just on our relationship for now, though I appreciate how much you want this. Start looking into other things, and I'll be there to support you. I do think that living together makes things a bit complicated, and I'm your tenant—"

"We should talk about that, how we pay for expenses—"

"Later. Just…about my family. I never tell them about the people I date right at the beginning. It's always at least a month or two. And I know things are complicated with Vince—"

"I want you to want to tell him, and for me to have the chance to say, 'No, let's wait.' I know that sounds ridiculous, but I can't help it."

He squeezes my hand. "I do want to tell them, but they'll freak out because we're roommates and they have a certain impression of you. Also, you may have known you were bi for decades, but I haven't. Even though they were accepting when I came out, a part of me fears it'll be different if I actually bring home someone who isn't a woman. That's why I was feeling them out by mentioning the same-sex relationship in my book, and it went well. But right now, our relationship feels like a cozy cocoon that most of the outside world doesn't touch, and I'm enjoying it." He runs his other hand through his hair, making it stand up more than usual. "Did it feel like I was ashamed of you? Or like I didn't believe it would work out?"

I look away, feeling foolish. "Yeah, I guess I thought you had no faith in my ability to maintain a relationship. Because you shouldn't."

"But I do," he says quietly. "I believe in you."

Like no one else ever has.

I'm used to being a disappointment, but that's not who I am to him.

"You're perfect," I whisper.

"I'm not, and you know it. I can be a bit clueless, but please never feel like you can't talk to me about these things. It's important to communicate."

I'm not the greatest at that, not in a deep, meaningful way, even if I have lots of friends. But at the same time, he makes me feel as if it's all possible.

"I think you assume I'm an expert at relationships," he says, "but just because I've had a few doesn't mean I'm completely at ease. I've had my heart broken before, and I can be a bit guarded because of that. In fact, I've been a little...overwhelmed by my feelings for you, but don't worry. I'm not going anywhere, and I'm not fighting what I feel."

"Oh," I say faintly, but inside, I'm smiling.

"Are we okay?" He wraps his arms around me. "We can talk about it more tomorrow. For now, I was thinking we could see the hedge maze."

"Because you're curious about hedge mazes? Or because you've never had a blowjob while surrounded by shrubbery?" My voice doesn't sound quite right. I don't have the casual, flirty tone that I usually manage without difficulty.

"Maybe it's a little of both. Not that we *have* to do anything, but..."

I'm tearing up a bit as I hug him back. I've never been such a mess of emotions before.

"We're okay," I say. "We'll figure it out over freshly baked cookies."

"I love you, you know. And not just for your baking skills."

Nobody has ever said those words to me before, and I swallow hard. "Love you, too."

He kisses my forehead, and we just stand there in Sam Leung's garden, soaking each other in. I'm dimly aware of the sounds of the party in the background, but this is what's important to me. My life with him.

We had our first fight—a small fight, but I think it would be hard to have a big fight with Cedric—and everything is okay.

And my guilt about breaking my promise to Vince has disappeared completely.

If Cedric wants to tell his family soon, I don't simply want the chance to say no; I want to say yes. We'll have to discuss the situation with Vince, but I don't want this to be a secret if it's okay with Cedric. At the same time, I understand how the last several weeks have been a lot for him, and I'm willing to wait. I get it.

And he loves me!

I'm so pleased.

I'm not going to fuck this up, but I also won't use it as an excuse to stop me from pursuing other things I want in life. I can do it, and I'm not the only person who believes that.

I glance around—we're still mostly hidden by the bush—before tugging Cedric closer, wanting a kiss before we explore the hedge maze together. His mouth opens for me immediately, and he's so warm and comforting, and everything I want…

And then someone grabs my shoulder and drags me out from behind the bush.

"What the hell?" says a familiar voice.

It's Vince.

[29]
CEDRIC

"You had one thing to do," Vince says, shaking Brian roughly. "I told you to keep your hands off my brother, and you couldn't even manage that?"

Oh, no.

There's going to be a fight because I kissed someone in Sam Leung's garden.

I'm not made for this level of drama. I prefer drama in the pages of a book or on screen. Not in real life.

"Stop it." I try to pull Vince back. "It's not what you think."

"It isn't?" he says.

"Why the hell are you acting like you're my older brother when you're younger than me? I was the one who had to lie to *you* when I learned Santa Claus wasn't real. I was the more responsible one who needed to keep an eye on you."

"No, Julian was—"

"Is it because I'm the only one who isn't married?" I ask. "Or because I'm not straight and you don't like the idea of men treating me the way you used to treat women?"

"I was never—"

"Why the hell are you here anyway? I thought you were done with partying."

"Sam invited me, and I figured I could use a night out."

Vince has relaxed slightly, but he's still tense. I pull his hands off Brian.

I haven't been this annoyed with my brother in decades, not since the infamous Nintendo incident of 1993.

"I tried to never be a piece of shit to women," Vince said. "Really. But I was all about casual encounters. No-strings-attached sex, and he was exactly the same." He jabs his finger in Brian's direction. "And that's not your style, Cedric, so it seemed like a bad idea. I didn't want you to get hurt."

"But then you found the right person," Brian says. "And I did, too." He looks at me, just for a split second, but it's enough to convey so much fondness. Love. He turns back to Vince. "To be clear, that person isn't you; it's Cedric. You told me not to 'screw around' with him, and I didn't. We've been together for over a month. If I remember correctly, you also once told me that I deserved someone who returned my feelings. But, fine, if you want to punch me, go ahead if it'll make you feel better." He gestures toward his face.

There's a shout, and I suddenly remember there are more than three of us here. I look around and notice everyone in the garden is staring at us. In the shadows, I see Sam Leung, wearing an inscrutable expression. I half expect him to step in, but he doesn't.

I throw myself in front of Brian because Vince wouldn't dare punch me, and a moment later, Carrie comes running down the slope, followed by Kris, who looks slightly disheveled.

Carrie pulls on Vince's arm. "You think Marissa would want you to throw a punch?"

"Did you know about this?" Vince asks her.

"Yes! Don't you think they're cute together?"

"Cedric, you can move, it's okay," Brian says.

I shake my head. "You did nothing wrong."

"Really, if it'll make him feel better, it's worth it."

"It won't make him feel better," I protest, "and you'll get blood on your suit. It's a nice suit. What if he breaks your nose?"

Brian shrugs, which makes Carrie gasp.

"Alright." Vince finally steps back and looks at me. "He's really treating you well?"

"Yes," I say.

"Then what were you and Brian arguing about, just a few minutes ago?" Kelvin asks.

Oh, for fuck's sake. Why is everyone watching?

Vince is tense again, which is alarming. He's usually much more easygoing.

"We had some slight communication problems. Everything's fine now." I direct this at my brother, even if it was Kelvin's question, and try to ignore the crowd. "Part of it was about telling you and the rest of the family. I wasn't entirely comfortable with the idea."

"For obvious reasons," Kris mutters, looking darkly at Vince.

"But it's out of my hands now," I say, "since there's no way Mom or Po Po won't hear about this within the next twelve hours."

Vince just stares at me for a moment before breaking into a familiar grin. "You'll probably get a phone call by nine in the morning, and if you don't pick up, Po Po will demand someone drive her right over."

"And I hope," I say quietly—I don't need this unwanted audience to hear everything, "they'll be okay with it. Me dating a man. This particular man."

I knew my parents supported LGBTQ rights, but I'd heard many stories of such parents not accepting their own child when they came out. So, I was nervous to tell my family, but it went okay, though as I told Brian, I'm still nervous about bringing him home.

Vince pulls me into a hug. A bunch of people in the crowd clap, someone whistles, and someone says, "Aww."

Me? I'm kinda embarrassed. Having an audience isn't really my thing.

Vince lets go of me, then slaps Brian on the back and gives him a hug. He whispers something in Brian's ear, but I can't hear what.

I look around the garden. People are going back to whatever they were doing before, thank God. Carrie squeezes my hand, and Kris pats my shoulder.

"You enjoying the party?" I ask her, and she laughs.

It's several minutes before Brian and I are alone again. Well, not really alone, but my brother and our friends have drifted away. He takes my hand and leads me toward the hedge maze. As we wind through the dark paths, it's rather thrilling and—

"Oh…oh…oh!"

Brian smiles, then leads me down another path, where nobody is making out.

"How do you know this maze so well?" I whisper.

"I've spent a bit of time here. At parties in the past."

We stop at a dead end and sit down on the small bench.

"Do you miss it?" I ask him. "Your old life? Your mansion?"

"I miss some things. I had a sunroom at the back of my house, plus a nice garden. It was peaceful when I wasn't having a party."

"Do you miss your hedge maze?"

He laughs. "Not especially." He takes my face in his hands. "Don't worry. I like my new life with you, very much, and now I have new things I want to try."

"What about all the orgies? Sleeping with lots of different people?"

He shakes his head. "I don't want that anymore, I promise. It's lost its appeal." And with that, he kisses me slowly, reverently, and my attention is entirely focused on him.

I think we're going to do lots of wonderful things together.

I hold him close and kiss him, a kiss that feels like a promise for our future.

~

The next morning, I wake to my phone ringing. I curse as I grab it from the bedside table.

"You're dating Brian Poon?" Po Po shouts.

"Please," I say, "it's first thing in the morning. You're giving me a headache."

"How many drugs did you do last night? Did you eat any special dumplings?"

I don't bother answering that. "Yes, Brian and I are together, and it's going well, thank you for asking, and he hasn't been a bad influence on me, don't worry."

Po Po sniffs. "I suppose I can believe it. He can't be too bad of an influence if you are writing a great book about me."

"The book isn't about *you*. For the last time."

Next to me, Brian laughs sleepily, and I find that sleep-roughened laugh rather arousing, even though I'm on the phone with my grandmother.

"I hear Vince punched Brian and broke his nose? Is Brian pressing charges?"

That's my mother. Are they on speakerphone, or has she wrestled the phone away from my grandmother?

"I don't know who your source is," I say, "but they're wrong. Vince *nearly* punched Brian, but fortunately, we managed to convince him not to do it."

"Oh, that's good," Mom says. "Vince's hand would hurt a lot if he threw a punch."

That's her concern? She's probably joking, but...

"It's too early in the morning for this," I mutter.

"Fine, fine, I'll let you go back to sleep."

I swear she's putting air quotes around "sleep."

"Wait," I say. "You're okay with Brian and me?"

"I just want you to be happy, honey. You sound cranky right now, but are you happy?"

"Yes. Very happy."

"Well, then I'm happy for you," she says. "Why don't you bring Brian to dinner next Sunday? We'd be glad to have him."

"Okay. I'll ask him. Just don't give him a hard time."

"I'll do my best, but I make no promises for other members of this household."

"Cedric!" Po Po is back on the phone. "You are bringing Brian for dinner tonight?"

"We aren't having a family dinner tonight. Next Sunday."

"I don't want to wait until next Sunday."

"But I thought Mom and Dad had plans tonight."

"I will demand they cancel them. They will have to listen to me. I am old."

"Ma!" my mother shouts in the background.

"You know," Po Po says, "it is thanks to me that you and Brian are together. Who suggested bachelor auction to your father? Who told you to be in it? Who bribed you with dumplings?"

Brian wraps his arms around me and nuzzles my neck. It's a little ticklish.

"Why are you laughing?" Po Po asks. "Did I say something funny?"

A few minutes later, I finally manage to get off the phone.

"You're invited to dinner next weekend," I tell Brian. "Would you like to come?"

He nods, and then he pulls me closer and kisses me. We have more things to talk about, but they can wait.

I run my hands up and down his body—naked except for his underwear—reveling in the fact that I get to touch him like this and have him all to myself. I reach between his legs and discover some impressive morning wood. As I grasp his erection, we both release a shuddering breath. He's so pretty when he starts to come undone.

I stroke him a few times before he grasps my cock. His gaze stays focused on mine.

Fuck, I need him in my mouth.

We didn't do this last night, as I decided a blowjob in a hedge maze wasn't something I needed to experience after all, but this morning…

I push back the blankets and remove his last scrap of clothing, admiring him in the morning light that filters into the bedroom. His skin is a touch paler than mine, and he's lean and beautiful. And between his legs…

I take him into my mouth, loving the gasp he makes as I do so. I wrap my hand around the base of his cock and suck on him in the way he likes—I've become an expert on his body in the last several weeks, and I want to become even more of an expert. To know every little part of him and build our lives together.

I release his cock with a *pop*, only to swirl my tongue around the head before diving back down. I adjust my position and reach between my legs with my other hand to stroke myself. When I glance up, his gaze is laser-focused on what I'm doing to pleasure both of us. He runs his hand through my hair, pulling just a little.

"Yeah, that's good," he murmurs.

I take him particularly deep, and he groans and grips the sheets.

"Cedric, I…"

He fills my mouth, and with a couple more strokes, I'm coming, too.

We clean ourselves up, and then I lie next to him and sling my arm around him.

"Was that a good way to start the morning?" I ask.

"Always. Now, how about I make some muffins and coffee?"

"Not yet. We'll stay here a bit longer, just because we can."

He runs his hand down to palm my ass. "I suppose I can get behind that."

We're quiet for several minutes, just lying in bed and basking in each other, but eventually we're interrupted by my phone ringing.

Surprisingly, it's not my family.

"Spencer?" I say into the phone.

"I conducted some important research for you last night," he tells me. "The pot pot stickers were *awesome*. I may have eaten too many. Want to come over next weekend and I'll make you some?"

After a brief chat with Spencer, I set the phone to silent then return to snuggling Brian.

I certainly never expected this when we went on our first "date," but there it is. Unexpected things can happen in real life, just like an unexpected person turns out to be the murderer in my book…

[30]

BRIAN

"I KNEW IT!" Winnie says when I tell her about Cedric that afternoon. "I knew you two were together, no matter how much you kept insisting otherwise."

"We weren't actually together then." I flop down on the couch. "But we are now."

"Details. When you visit us in August, you should bring him."

"Alright. I suspect he'll be happy to come."

We talk for a little longer, and I'm just ending the call when Cedric opens the door, returning from his walk. I smile when I see him. He's stopped to check the mail on the way up—we don't get many letters, so we only check it a couple of times a week— and he hands me an envelope. I take it, hands shaking when I see the handwriting, and even though there's no return address, I can tell that Cedric knows who it's from. He sits beside me on the couch and turns me so he can rub my shoulders.

"It's your birthday?" he asks when he sees the card.

"Not for more than a week, but I guess she wanted to make sure I got it in time."

Yes, it's a birthday card from my mother, and I can't help

sobbing. I don't miss my brother and dad, but she's the one who raised me, and I do miss her.

Cedric holds me close and wipes the tears from my cheeks, but he doesn't tell me to stop crying. And just having someone here for me like this… It's everything.

My mother might not be part of my life right now, but I have other people, ones I've chosen for myself.

Including, best of all, Cedric Fong.

"You look tired today," Vince says to Julian. "Did Evie have a bad night?"

"Me!" Evie says, and her father pulls her onto his lap.

Cedric, Julian, and I are sitting on the couch in the Fongs' living room. Vince is on an armchair, Lucas asleep in his arms.

I've met everyone here before—except Evie—but this is the first time I'm meeting them as Cedric's boyfriend, which is a little frightening, I'm not going to lie. They weren't going to have a family dinner tonight, but I guess his grandma got her way after all.

"No, sweetie, it wasn't you," Julian says to his daughter. "You slept well, after you literally spent an hour running in circles in the backyard." He turns to Vince. "I got a call at one in the morning from Kelvin Kwong. He told me that my brothers were in a fight and I should come break it up."

"He *called* you?" Cedric asks.

"Unfortunately. Then he called back three minutes later, as I was starting to get dressed, to say you'd hugged it out."

"You were really going to come over to Sam Leung's?"

"It was the first time I'd gotten a call about the two of you fighting, so it seemed serious. I don't remember you physically fighting since grade school, and that was over a videogame."

"Don't blame me," Cedric says. "Vince was the one who wanted to throw punches."

Julian turns to me. "So, uh, Brian." He scratches his head, as though struggling to think of something we might have in common—and I get it. Julian is a father and the CEO of an investment company. He's nothing like me. "Vince tells me you took up baking?"

"His biscotti are surprisingly good," Vince says.

"I did try to make biscotti once." Julian's lips quirk. "I figured Courtney would enjoy one with her gingerbread latte, but I burnt them."

"He did something that wasn't perfect." Vince puts a hand to his mouth. "Call the press!"

"Oh, shut up," Julian mutters.

"Shut up!" Evie repeats.

He covers her ears. "Evie had a meltdown while the biscotti were in the oven because she couldn't find her favorite Cookie Monster toy."

"Was it left out in the backyard?" Vince asks. "Did it get run over by a lawnmower?"

"No, Cookie Monster had apparently decided to hide behind the couch."

Cedric takes out his phone. "Well, Brian didn't burn his biscotti. He also made me this." There's pride in his voice, and he shows Julian a picture. "Chocolate fudge cake with praline buttercream. Too bad there was none for you. It was really good."

Evie stares at the photo, as though deep in concentration, then walks across her father's and uncle's laps until she reaches me. She pokes my shoulder with her tiny finger.

When Courtney enters the room, Evie tries to jump off the couch, but I hold her back, then set her down on the floor. She runs to her mother and points to me. "Brrr."

"Yes, there's a new person here. It's Brian. Should we wave at him?"

Evie waves.

"Evie likes him because she thinks he's going to make her a cake," Vince says.

"Cake!" she exclaims.

It's different seeing Vince with his family rather than out at parties. I still feel slightly awkward with him, and I know I'm quieter than usual—meeting a partner's family isn't something I've done before. But I feel like I can figure it out.

"One day," I say to Evie, "I can make you a Cookie Monster cake. What do you think?"

She runs back to me and throws her arms around my leg, and I laugh. Nothing is going to change my mind about having kids, but I think this is going to be fun.

Evie spreads her arms wide. "Big cake."

"Maybe not *that* big."

I'm about to say something else to her, but then I'm distracted by Courtney and Cedric's conversation.

"…ask Naomi if she'd be willing to talk to Brian about event planning?" Cedric says.

"Of course." Courtney smiles at me. "I'm sure she'd be happy to do that."

"Thank you," I say. "I appreciate it."

At dinner, Cedric's grandma asks me to sit beside her.

"I don't know if he needs to be subjected to that," Cedric says.

"Aiyah!" she exclaims. "I will be nice, I promise. But he is going to tell me all the secrets in your book. Who is poisoning who!"

"I haven't read it yet," I tell her.

"Hmph. Why not?"

Cedric looks at me. "I'm not ready, and Brian respects that. But one day."

"Yes," I say, my voice suddenly scratchy. "One day."

~

That night, Cedric and I are reading in bed together when his phone buzzes.

Ten minutes later, he's still texting up a storm.

"What's up?" I ask. "Is your family unimpressed with me?"

I'm joking. Mostly. I think I did a decent job at the meet-the-parents business. His grandma even offered to teach me how to make her dumpling recipe, and when I said yes, Julian, Cedric, and Vince looked at me like I was making the biggest mistake of my life. Apparently, her lessons are intense, and Vince didn't last five minutes.

"No, it's not my family." Cedric kisses me on the cheek before going back to texting.

He's being unusually secretive. I don't want to be insecure about this, but I can't help feeling like he's talking about me behind my back.

I return to reading, but when I've spent ten minutes staring at the same page, Cedric leans over and rests his head on my shoulder.

"This is supposed to be a secret," he says, "but I think it's making you uncomfortable, so I'm going to tell you. We're planning your birthday party."

"We?"

"Kris, Michael, Ted, and I."

I'm touched. No one has done something like this for me before. Back in the day, I was famous for throwing my own wild birthday parties.

His phone buzzes, and he picks it up and laughs before turning it toward me.

I shut my eyes. "I don't need to know the details of the party. Those can be a surprise."

"This isn't about the party. Ginny must have gotten her hands on Michael's phone."

Cedric shows me goat gif after goat gif, and we laugh together.

My life isn't as glamorous as it used to be, but I'm sure as hell not complaining.

[EPILOGUE]

CEDRIC

IT'S MONDAY FEBRUARY 16, and tonight, we're celebrating our sixth Valentine's Day.

Brian is quite busy with his event-planning business, and he had an event on February 14, so we couldn't celebrate then. The weekend before, it was the gala for the Toronto Chinese Canadian Center, which his business now handles. The charity bachelor auction was discontinued a few years ago, however, following a highly dramatic and slightly violent incident with sweet red bean soup, during bidding for a date with Kelvin Kwong. But Brian and I make sure to donate a good amount of money each year.

We've been together for a little less than five years, since we didn't actually start dating right after the bachelor auction, though Valentine's Day was the day he asked me to move in with him.

We've lived together ever since.

We're no longer in the same building, though. We both decided we wanted a house. Nothing like what Brian had before, but something a little bigger than the condo. Last year, we bought a semi-detached Victorian in the Annex, and the third-floor room facing the street is my office.

Since quitting my teaching job two years ago, I've been writing full-time. I'm now on the eighth book in my cozy mystery series, with a new series set to debut next fall. After years of barely writing, it's amazing that I can now write two books a year.

I check my watch. It's almost nine thirty, and I've been up here working for a couple of hours after dinner.

Time to head out.

After getting dressed, I walk quickly to the southeast, to where I'm meeting Brian for our date. He's had lots of long days lately, but for the rest of tonight and tomorrow, neither of us is doing any work.

When I arrive at Lychee, I make my way to the second floor. It's not too busy tonight, probably owing to the fact that it's a Monday, though it is Family Day and many people have a three-day weekend.

It's easy to find Brian. My gaze is immediately drawn to him in any room, in any situation. And he's definitely the most handsome and well-dressed person here.

"Happy dateaversary." I kiss him on the cheek before sitting down across from him and taking off my coat.

"You, too."

"Hope you haven't been waiting long."

"Just long enough to read over the special drinks menu for the Lunar New Year. We should order some food, too. I didn't eat dinner."

I give him a look.

"I know, I know," he says. "It's hard getting a business off the ground, but it won't always be like this." He worked at a couple of different places in preparation for striking out on his own, and I'm proud of what he's accomplished.

I squeeze his leg under the table. "We'll get you some char siu sliders." I scan the special drinks. "I'll have the spiced persimmon cocktail."

"Me, too." He smiles at me then fixes my misbehaving hair.

We've been married for almost two years. Our wedding wasn't a totally over-the-top affair like something out of *Crazy Rich Asians*, but it was still a grand party because that's what Brian wanted. He, naturally, did more of the planning than I did, though no one planned on Evie calling the officiant "Santa Claus" after she sprinkled flower petals down the aisle.

But nothing ever goes exactly as planned, which Brian is intimately aware of. He has to put out fires on a regular basis at his job. (I mean, not *literal* fires—except for that one time.)

I guess you could say it started with dumplings, since they're the reason I agreed to the bachelor auction. Though I no longer need my grandma to make dumplings because Brian, after many lessons and much yelling, finally managed to perfect Po Po's dumplings. Which is good, as her hands are no longer as nimble as they once were. She's gotten frailer, but she's still here with us, living with my parents and occasionally calling me at inconvenient moments. Whenever she thinks of an idea for one of my books, she calls me right away so that she doesn't forget it. She's very invested in my series.

Spencer still makes his pot pot stickers, too. They're not as delicious as Brian's dumplings, although they do have other benefits.

There's no awkwardness between Vince and Brian anymore, much to my relief, and they're good friends again. Vince and Marissa have a daughter now, and Julian and Courtney have another daughter, too—the girls are only three months apart. Brian and I, however, are still happy with our decision not to have kids.

The server returns with our drinks, which are served in... What on earth? I'd thought they might come in giant persimmon glasses, something exciting like that, but instead?

Regular lowball glasses.

I start laughing, and Brian smiles at me as he clinks his glass against mine.

"They changed their menu recently," he says. "They got rid of the Wild Beary, and lightbulb glasses are a little passé."

"But—"

"Don't worry, I've got a surprise for you tomorrow." He winks.

The next day, we have a leisurely morning in bed, and Brian makes my favorite muffins. He doesn't bake as much as he used to, but we still have breakfast together every morning, although usually we're in more of a rush. It's nice to feel like we have all the time in the world today. I give him a small box of chocolates from Peony, which we eat very, very slowly in the midst of other activities.

For lunch, we go out, but for dinner, we have a cozy meal of dumplings at home, plus…

I peer at my drink, served in a familiar vessel.

A bear's head.

"How did you…?"

Brian leans back in his chair, enjoying my surprise. "I have my ways." He waggles his eyebrows before leaning forward and sliding his hand up my thigh.

I might be used to his touch, but I never tire of it, and it can still make my heart race.

"I know you do," I murmur, and then I kiss him, this man who can make amazing dumplings and blueberry orange muffins. This man who has done so much for me, this man whom I intend to be with for always.

My husband.

ACKNOWLEDGMENTS

Thank you to my editor, Latoya C. Smith, for helping me make this book the best it could be. I would also like to thank Ceillie Simkiss and Emerson Blake for their help with the manuscript, and my Facebook reader group for their help with the title. The lovely cover was created by Flirtation Designs.

And thank you to Toronto Romance Writers, plus my husband and father, for all your support.

ABOUT THE AUTHOR

Jackie Lau decided she wanted to be a writer when she was in grade two, sometime between writing "The Heart That Got Lost" and "The Land of Shapes." She later studied engineering and worked as a geophysicist before turning to writing romance novels. Jackie lives in Toronto with her husband, and despite living in Canada her whole life, she hates winter. When she's not writing, she enjoys gelato, gourmet donuts, cooking, hiking, and reading on the balcony when it's raining.

To learn more and sign up for her newsletter,
visit jackielaubooks.com.

ALSO BY JACKIE LAU

Donut Fall in Love

The Stand-Up Groomsman

Cider Bar Sisters Series

Her Big City Neighbor

His Grumpy Childhood Friend

Her Pretend Christmas Date (novella)

The Professor Next Door

Her Favorite Rebound

Her Unexpected Roommate

Kwan Sisters/Fong Brothers Series

Grumpy Fake Boyfriend

Mr. Hotshot CEO

Pregnant by the Playboy

Bidding for the Bachelor

Holidays with the Wongs Series

A Match Made for Thanksgiving

A Second Chance Road Trip for Christmas

A Fake Girlfriend for Chinese New Year

A Big Surprise for Valentine's Day

Baldwin Village Series

One Bed for Christmas (prequel novella)

The Ultimate Pi Day Party

Ice Cream Lover

Man vs. Durian

Chin-Williams Series

Not Another Family Wedding

He's Not My Boyfriend

www.ingramcontent.com/pod-product-compliance
Lightning Source LLC
Chambersburg PA
CBHW051221210726

48290CB00003B/738